I0693200

LOST IN THE DARK

A Short Story Collection

A V IAIN

Contents

HARD TIMES FOR KINDER CORNERS

1

I N THE SEWERS everything was much clearer.

Even, at twenty-seven years old, Roger saw that.

Maybe he would become a great philosopher after all.

The rancid sweet smell was the great equaliser, because, with that smell, it was no longer necessary to think. There was nothing else apart from the putrid, full-blooded odour. And if you got to thinking anything else then there was no doubt that you were dead.

Cold.

Hard.

Dead.

He shifted his weight onto his other leg, the leg that he hadn't broken when he'd got hit by the truck last week. He had gone to the hospital. He had sat there, on the plastic seats, and he'd watched on as the people—the waiting *patients*—had screwed up their noses, had been *repulsed* by his odour. And he had wanted nothing more than to return to the sewers, to find himself back down here.

Sensory deprivation, he felt, was underrated.

The doctors—or maybe it had been the nurses—had patched him up okay. They'd put this cast onto his leg so that it would mend with time. They'd asked him to come back for an appointment on some date, though that information had escaped him almost as soon as it had left their lips.

How could he have a concept of time?

In the sewers there *was* no time.

He limped his way along the concrete tunnel, keeping out of the trickling creek of rubbish juice which ran down the centre. He eyed the light beaming in. That grapefruit-pink glow that he knew to recognise as daybreak.

Not that it would matter much.

He would spend the day down here, in the sewers.

Night-time was *his* domain.

Still, he did love to watch the sun dawn on the world, he loved to watch it tickle the rooftops, and, most of all, he loved to feel it warm his chest.

To say that the sun had a restorative effect on him was to put it very mildly indeed.

He thought of himself now, in his current guise, as being something more resembling a cold-blooded being. He needed the sun to give him energy—to give him *life*.

Without it, he would be nothing.

Nothing more than a husk.

A scrap of human skin somehow propped apart by rutted—and *broken*—bones.

When he reached the tunnel, he looked on out, over the world.

All was not right today. He could see that at a glance.

The yellow tape which hung about the concrete patch leading up to the tunnel. The way that it had been *cordoned* off. And he could make out several men, all of them wearing yellow hats, and with yellow fluorescent strips on their otherwise grey overalls.

What did they want here?

What did they want with the sewer?

He counted out the men in his mind—just as a lord in ancient times might've counted out the enemy horsemen from a nearby vantage point. He soon picked out their leader.

Leaders of this sort were easy to spot.

It was the man who, like the others, wore a grey overall. But, through the unzipped neck of his overall, Roger caught sight of the shirt and tie beneath. And that was without even thinking about the way the man held himself. How he stood as if he had a wooden board stuck up the back of his shirt.

He knew he was better.

That he was superior.

Roger knew their kind.

And he had grown to fear them.

A little way beyond the men, he spotted their lorry.

In some aspects, it resembled a cement mixer, all except for the fact that it had a hose attachment stuck onto its side. One of those flexible tubes which was designed to be stuck into the trickiest of nooks, or the subtlest of crannies. To pump it full of water, and who knew what else.

Thinking quickly, and without the men having noticed him, he retreated into the tunnel.

And back into the darkness.

2

ROGER'S EYES quickly adapted to the dark. This was his home, after all. It was a part of him. He came across the slumped-up form. He bent down, gave the form a slight nudge in the side. He felt the warm bundle of human life stir.

Fiona.

"Hey," he said. "Hey?"

The bundle stirred a little more still. Then murmured something.

He crouched down, knowing that there really wasn't all that much time. "Come on," he said. "We have to go."

". . . Wha . . .?" the bundle said, the silhouette of a neck and head emerging from the gloom.

"Some men," he said, and this time he laid hands on her, decided that they needed to really get moving now. He helped her all the way back onto her feet.

She couldn't walk straight without stumbling all over the place, so he had to support her.

It was agony for his broken leg.

They had maybe got about twenty paces along the tunnel, heading in the opposite direction to the mouth which the men all occupied, when he thought he was hearing things. He stopped, stayed stock still.

"Wha . . . is it?" Fiona said, beside him.

And it was then he knew it was too late.

That there was nothing they could do now.

All he could do was look over his shoulder and watch the gushing water burst along what had once been nothing more than a flimsy weak little trickle of water.

It was like a tidal wave.

Just before it struck, he tugged Fiona to his chest. And said a little prayer.

3

THE WATER KNOCKED Roger back to the ground. Broke off his contact with Fiona. She fell down into the gushing torrent also. He thrashed his limbs but they had no effect. He couldn't battle against this unstoppable flow, nor could he so much as change his direction.

He was, in short, a prisoner.

He felt the cast on his leg begin to melt away, as if it was nothing substantial at all. It hung to him like a damp blister that demanded to be cut free. But he had no opportunity to do so. He and his cast needed to be carried along on this torrent.

The water burned his skin, and he caught the strong scent of chemicals clambering up his nose.

Seeming to singe his nostril hair.

He scrabbled all the more, but, in doing so, he found himself opening his mouth to breathe.

And he took some of the water in.

That burned too. This time, though, rather than his skin, it burned his tongue and throat. It seemed to strip any taste that had once resided inside his mouth.

He choked and tried to push his focus back onto his staying afloat in the gush of water. But even this was difficult now. The torrent was so forceful. It almost reached the concrete ceiling of the underground sewer. He could feel himself thrown about like a ragdoll.

His leg flared with hot needle-sharp pain all over. He crunched his teeth together to try and take his mind off it, but that only worked for a couple of moments before the ravishing pain returned and, despite the brutal flow of water, tears of pain leaked out from around his eyes.

Now his task became more one of taking pain. Of absorbing all the pain he could manage. As the water tossed him along, he felt his legs crunch beneath him, fold up on themselves. Several times he felt acute pain in his toes.

Were they breaking?

He had no time to blink away old pains before fresh ones descended on him.

Before he found himself—once more—crushed up against the concrete wall of the sewer.

It wasn't long after that he felt his body go limp, not with death, at least he hoped not, but with something like fatigue. He simply had nothing more within him. None of that 'inner steel' everybody around him had once told him he possessed in spades.

For the first time in his life, he felt like giving up.

. . . *No*, he *was* giving up.

A conscious decision.

And once he'd made it, he felt like he was floating along on a cloud.

For the first time ever *really* free.

Ten Years Before

ROGER COULD FEEL his heart pounding. His mouth still tasted of shit, even though he'd spent fifteen minutes brushing his teeth with that disgusting fruity toothpaste.

He felt stupid—*stiff*—wearing this suit and tie. He was over-dressed, he was certain about it. And yet he knew, really, if he ever *was* going to be overdressed then this was the time to do it. What might be the most important night of his life . . . of *both* of their lives. His and Fiona's.

In his jacket pocket he could feel the weight of the ring—all snug there, inside its box. He thought back about half an hour, about how he had, somehow, become fixated on the idea the box might have some micro hole within it. That, on the short walk over here, to Fiona's house, the ring might somehow conspire to rub itself up against the boundaries of the box and open up a tear.

And then the ring would slip out.

And, in its same *mystical* ways, it would break through a previously undiscovered, raggedy hole in his jacket pocket. But he could feel the ring box still snug there.

It would be okay.

It was *all* going to be okay.

He stared at the door. At its thick blue coating, recently touched up. Not only paint itself, but a layer of varnish too. He dizzily thought about how Fiona's father wouldn't be having any trouble with the fierce winter predicted. The one which just about every newspaper had cottoned onto, and had unoriginally dubbed the 'Big Freeze'.

But, despite this prediction, he could feel the muggy night drawing around him like a wet, mouldy blanket.

From within the house, he could hear the scrub of footsteps against carpet, and he knew, as he felt his heart swelling in his throat, that he only had moments to wait. Another couple of seconds. He kept up that intense stare, and watched the door open in on itself.

Fiona appeared on the front porch. Today she wore a white blouse over a pair of tight black jeans. He could make out the outline of the black bra she wore underneath.

For a few seconds, he couldn't help mindlessly—in that testosterone-pumped, teenage way—drinking in the curves of her body, and thinking about what lay beneath. His little secret. That was what he told himself. The only one Fiona had shown her body to.

And that was how it would be for the rest of their lives.

They were soulmates.

Nothing more to it.

They walked along the pavement in silence, not because they had nothing to say, but because they didn't need to so much as speak to share their feelings. A benefit of being kindred hearts.

When they'd got about a street away from her house, Roger knew there was no way he would be able to get through the whole of dinner with the secret concealed within his jacket pocket. It would make him jittery. He would find himself sweating all over—mangling words . . . and he knew that Fiona would cotton on, subconsciously, that there was something the matter with him.

It would blow his surprise *anyway*.

And so, right there, on the corner of her street, with the odd car humming by, and the thick bushy fern trees billowing in the evening breeze, he got down on one knee.

He asked her.

She said yes.

4

ROGER'S MIND was escaping him. Even as it happened, he could recognise it for what it was.

His body—his *human* body—could no longer take the abuse it was suffering.

It was shutting down.

He wondered if what was happening to him was an 'out-of-body' experience.

Was he rising up now?

Could he see his body down below him, in the third-person?

Or was he caught somewhere between desperation and unlimited fatigue?

He continued to jet along with the swell of the chemical-inflected water.

No longer did it burn his skin. He had made peace with the fact that—never again—would he taste another thing. That he would never smell another thing. It was only when he could hear his own thoughts that he realised that the rushing water had made him deaf.

All that was around him now was the grey water.

Grey.

Flimsy.

Almost like a cloud . . .

R OGER BROUGHT his finger down hard on the sticky button. The button on the till that he always had trouble with. As he felt the concealed ancient springs within the till bend, he waited for the giveaway *ting!* before reaching down, automatically, for the sliding drawer which emerged.

He scooped change into his hand, listened to it jangle, and then he handed it over to the customer: an old silver-haired lady in her seventies or eighties.

As he poured the coins out into her wrinkled leathery hand, she gave him a bright blue-eyed smile. He cast a quick glance over that light pink lipstick of hers, those slightly moist lips, and then she trod out of the shop.

It seemed that here, in this tiny village where he and Fiona lived, they were surrounded by these old ladies. Widows, every last one of them. All alone now. Often while in some sort of a daze during one of his long afternoon shifts, he would find himself speculating what might happen to Fiona, whether she might end up in a similar situation.

That was the thing about life expectancy.

Women outlived *men*.

In his more profound moments, he had squared this concept with the idea of immortality, because that was surely what it was in a way. What was immortality but that time when everybody around you was gone . . . when everything was changed . . .

What was the difference between being five years past your own generation and being a hundred years past it?

Oftentimes, Mr Kwan, the owner of the village shop, would catch Roger unawares. He was one of those people who had the habit of sneaking up silently and observing. Whenever he saw fit to break in, to make Roger aware of his presence, he would always say something along the lines of, 'Away with fairies?' in an idiomatic way which clashed with his accented English.

Roger would then, without exception, blink away his daze and look to his boss.

And Mr Kwan would simply slip away once again, shaking his head and smiling to himself.

The kindly old man spent his spare time seeing to his sickly wife who stayed in bed all day. He was a good boss, probably the best Roger had ever had. He trusted him implicitly, and never questioned these little flights of fantasy. And that made it all the harder knowing what he had to do.

What he had to do for himself and Fiona.

As he listened to the clapped-out bell above the door let out its dull *clang!*, he worked quickly, snatched up all the cash he could get from the till. He slipped it into his trouser pocket, and then, looking around, he ducked down below the counter to where the safe was concealed.

Today was the day that the money would be collected.

A *Thursday*.

A secure van would soon show up to take the money away.

Roger had already put off this robbery twice before. He had first discussed it with Fiona about a month ago, and they had decided, with mounting bills, and their new-born baby—*Joe*—to feed, that there was simply no other way.

The money which Roger earned from his minimum-wage shifts wouldn't keep them afloat any longer. The loans were being called back. They would be unceremoniously tossed from their house in a matter of days.

As he typed the code into the safe—the code which Mr Kwan had trusted him with—he felt a slight swelling of his heart. He knew that stealing was wrong.

Knew it deep down, right to the pit of his gut.

And yet, at the same time, he knew that there was nothing else to be done.

The only chance that he and his wife, Fiona, and their son, had of getting away was a clean break.

And for that clean break they'd need money.

The safe sprang open. The heavy door bounced outward.

Roger worked quickly, not stopping to count the money.

There was no time.

He stuffed all the cash he could into his trouser pocket, and then, after looking about the shop, checking to see if Mr Kwon might be standing silently in a corner—*he wasn't*—Roger slipped out for the last time. He had only trodden about five paces before he couldn't resist the adrenalin rush.

He broke into a run.

He fled to them.

To his fledgling family.

Already feeling the tears prickle in his eyes.

5

T HE WATER was more like a swell now.

Keeping Roger afloat.

Simply carrying him along.

He knew that now, if he had wanted to, if he'd had the energy, he could've paddled this way or that, but he *didn't* have the energy.

In fact, he felt like he was dead.

If Fiona was gone that would be the end.

He decided that now.

Consciously.

Though the water continued to wash along beneath him, Roger could feel that it was now getting to the point where he would be able to stand upright. Where he would be able to plant his feet, taking care with his broken leg which now felt numb.

But he had nothing.

Nothing left to give.

And so he simply allowed the current to take him.

In his mind, he thought of the thing as a sort of spiritual journey, almost like one of those native-American passages through darkness, through sensory deprivation.

He found himself laughing giddily, those strange *foreign* barks coming back at him off the cement walls which surrounded him.

What did he look like now?

He supposed that he must look something of a monster.

Like a half-man.

He wondered how—at some stage earlier in his life—he had walked proud, kept his chin up.

Shown all of them.

And then life's little series of misfortunes, those punches to the gut, had come along like a never-ending stream. One misfortune after another. He had begun to lose faith.

. . . But when Joe died, when the life left their son . . .

That was the 'straw that broke the camel's back'.

And the image of the camel, being crushed beneath its own load, its knees buckling, head dipping down, eyes straining, seemed impossibly funny to Roger in that instant.

Because that camel was himself.

It might've been hours before he began to see daylight.

His whole body was wracked by a numbness that he had never previously experienced. When he felt the sunlight lick his skin, he somehow felt subhuman, like he would never find once more what had set him apart from an animal.

Was he worried about his pride?

No.

His appearance?

Neither.

Both of those things were long gone.

He simply floated along on the surface of the water, unable to bring himself to so much as turn his head, to look at the concrete banks as they passed him by.

He could only look up—*up to the sky.*

It was a beautiful day.

All blue.

A fluffy white cloud here and there.

And the freshness of the breeze which blew over him. That breeze which demonstrated to him just how overpowering the chemical stench—the chemical *taste*—had been within the sewer.

He breathed it into his trembling lungs.

He took it all down.

And he felt the air lifting him.

Keeping his head afloat.

Stopping him from sinking.

From drowning.

R OGER SQUEEZED the steering wheel of his newly bought estate car—the first *new* car that he had ever owned outright. He checked himself in the mirror, the podgy cheeks, the thinning hairline, and that base layer of grit that he guessed he would never quite be able to get himself shot of completely. Homelessness left a mark on a person.

A mark which lingered forever.

Just below the surface.

Sometimes, while he sat in this meeting, or that meeting, at work, he wondered what might happen if one of his colleagues decided to prick him with the sharp point of a ballpoint pen. Would all the grime—all of it absorbed over so many years—pool out of him?

Would it fill the meeting room, trickle onto the carpet, always rising till it reached their shoes, till it splattered up everybody's trouser legs?

He was glad nobody at work ever thought to jab his skin to see what might come out.

He sank down into the leather-upholstered driving seat, and he breathed in that fresh, clean, new-car smell. It was true what people said, there really was nothing else quite like it. Nothing so distinct. Nothing so life-affirming.

As he trundled around the corner, he found himself staring out at a familiar sight. Something which caught him off guard. He was so lost in the spectacle before him that he almost missed the lorry as it rose up over him, and he just swerved in time, yanking the car out of the way into the side of the road. The lorry blared its horn as it roared past.

But he didn't so much as look again at the lorry, his gaze was completely fixed on what had appeared to him.

An aqueduct.

Concreted sides.

And a narrow trickle of water down the centre.

He knew this place.

Of course he did.

This was where they had fished him out.

Then taken him to the hospital.

Made him better.

Asked him his name . . . and when he had lied . . . made himself a new life . . . a clean start . . . something to start over from.

He sat there, at the wheel, just staring out at the grim, grey concrete. And then, as if something well below his level of conscious thought had already decided it for him, he shifted away from beneath the steering wheel and stepped out onto the grassy—*slightly muddy*—verge.

He looked both ways before crossing the road.

———

As Roger strode along the concrete bank of the aqueduct, he found himself sniffing out that same chemical smell from before. Though his sense of smell wasn't much good these days, and his taste near non-existent, he could still catch a whiff of that chemical odour just fine.

Because he smelled it every day.

A shimmer passed over the surface of his skin, and the gentle trickle of the water at the base of the aqueduct sent chills through his blood.

He would've liked nothing more than to turn around, to get back in his car, and to drive away from all this . . . to drive away from his past . . . but he was unable.

When he *tried* to take a step back, he felt an almost magnetic repulsion preventing him.

He had to see.

He had thought of this for so long.

As he carried on his way, unaware of his destination, he caught sight of a tunnel up ahead. He wondered whether it might've been the same tunnel the water had blasted him out of . . . or perhaps, more likely from the way that the water flowed *into* it, this was the tunnel where he had been headed. If they hadn't fished him out, that would've been his future.

Right there.

As he stared into the darkness of the tunnel he slowly felt his mind crunching in on itself, as if the confines of his skull had suddenly just become too much for his brain to bear . . . but he was certain what he could see . . . what he saw emerging from the shadows.

A figure.

A *shadowy* figure.

Already, he could feel the tears coming, thick and warm and salty, but he didn't reach up to brush them away. Sometimes, as he had learned, he simply had to let the tears flow.

He stared at the figure, nothing more than a bundle of rags— just like that bundle of rags he had stirred, seemingly so many years ago.

In the overcast day, the slightly grim visibility, he almost missed the raised hand, the gesture to him, the *wave*. He stood there, on the bank of the aqueduct.

He waved back.

Then, feeling that the sensation which kept him pinned there had dissipated, he turned on his heel, and strode back toward his car.

It was like another life.

Another life entirely.

Just how many would he be permitted to live?

MEDIUMS OF THE MIDNIGHT MANSION

1

SITTING ON THE BACK SEAT of the beaten-up van and headed up the rutted dirt track leading up the hill to the mansion which sat on top, Josephine wondered if she was the only one there who was at all sceptical. The only one with any sense about her.

Though she could hardly sit still in her seat as the van bounced around—the springs of its suspension creaking in an alarming way —her hunger pangs overwhelmed anything else she might've been feeling, and, with her rucksack perched on her lap, she dug through for something to scavenge.

She finally came across a half-squished banana at the bottom. When she brought it out, the smell of banana was thick and, she was sure, filled the whole of the van. The banana had long ago turned black, but, as her father had always told her, 'Never let anything go to waste.' And so she peeled it back and chomped on the sweet fruit within. Already she felt a new-found warmth passing through her gut, getting right down to her bones. That was good. Enough to take her mind off these inane conversations. The conversations coming at her from all sides.

She peered out over the seats, to the heads which bounced along with each movement of the van. There were seven others packed into the van, in all, including the driver. Just a small crew. That had been sold to her as an advantage by her client. Her client had told her that she shouldn't have too much trouble getting access to everybody she needed.

But, already, seeing the mansion towering up above her, perched precariously onto the plateau of the barren hillside—long ago stripped of trees—she was already feeling greatly apprehensive. There was something about ghosts that she deeply disliked. And yet she had taken this job. She supposed, in a way, she wanted to prove something to herself, wanted to show her fleeting, fairy tale-believing self, once and for all, that there was *no such thing*.

Her client had sold himself to her as a mainstream sceptic—somebody who wanted proof for his next book on the subject of exposing mediums. Of course, as he had told her, he simply didn't have the time to investigate for himself, and, in any case, if *he* had shown up here with these people they would've been likely to drive him away with pitchforks.

If there was one thing that Josephine could easily agree with her client on, it was the fact that mediums—or anybody involved with the 'supernatural'—were extremely guarded of their 'connection' to the spiritual world.

The van jerked to the left and Josephine, neatly and gracefully, she thought, deposited the last of her banana in between her lips. She chewed on it pensively, staring out at the Victorian mansion that was now looming large above them.

It *did* seem dark and foreboding in the overcast daylight, and with night quickly storming in on the horizon. It made her glad that she had packed her extra-warm fleece, along with—not one, but *two* —winter coats.

It was certainly set up to be a long night, that was for sure.

Whether or not she saw any ghosties at all was a matter up for debate.

2

THE VAN CAME to a stop with a heaving *crunch* of tyres.

The driver hopped out of his seat up front and he walked around to slide open the side door with an ear-splitting *roar*.

As Josephine waited her turn to slip out of her seat, and to step down from the van, she noticed how it now felt like her ears had been stuffed with cotton wool from all grinding of the engine and the creaking of springs on the way up the uneven dirt path.

She blinked away her daze as soon as the last person left the seat in front of her, and, with a little more nimbleness than she felt, she leaped down and landed on the gravel driveway of the mansion.

Here she was, among the 'nuts' as her client had put it.

She looked about herself, already felt the crispy chill on the wind. She drew her rucksack up over her shoulder and felt its gentle weight—the soft shapes of her clothing nestled within.

She looked back down the dirt track, where they had come from, and she wondered whether anybody else would be coming by the mansion at any time this weekend.

It had been at least four or five miles up that dirt track, and it was almost a struggle to recall what smooth, tarmacked road really felt like.

Still, she guessed that she would find out in a week or so, when she went back home.

And hopefully with the information she needed for her client.

"Well, hello there!"

Josephine turned, found herself staring into the sapphire eyes of the medium, as she had been briefed by her client, who was called Alburton Neighbour. Well, to tell the truth, in the course of her researching this job, Josephine had watched several episodes of *Mediums of the Midnight Mansion*, so she did recognise him from those too.

Alburton was in his fifties, still had a full head of silver hair, and his skin was—almost unnaturally—smooth.

As Josephine accepted his outstretched hand, and gave his well-moisturised skin a good shake, she thought about how she'd believed Alburton's smooth skin, on the TV, had been down to good makeup and kind lighting.

Now, though, she was forced to reassess.

It must be plastic surgery.

Alburton clung to Josephine's hand for several seconds longer than was necessary, and he did that thing which really creeped Josephine out, whereby a man simply *refuses* to break off eye contact.

When Josephine finally got her hand back, and introduced herself as a journalist working for a fictitious magazine—the cover story her client had fed her—Alburton continued to hang around her like a bad odour.

The other five members of the team: another couple of psychics, a cameraman, a sound guy and the director, were all fairly uninterested in Josephine.

A little standoffish, in fact.

Though Josephine guessed that she couldn't blame them.

From their perspective she was an outsider, after all.

And, considering her goal, considering what her client was paying her to do, they had all the reason in the world to cast her out.

For twenty minutes, they stood about waiting for the caretaker: a man surely aged anywhere between seventy to a hundred. He arrived wearing a bulky, fleecy coat, and holding a heavy, jangling set of impossibly ancient keys.

Josephine always marvelled at the ability of country people to make themselves feel important—to make themselves feel *needed*.

Surely the caretaker had heard them coming, surely he could've ventured out from whatever tumbledown shack he called home and let them into the mansion . . . but, no, he had to show them whose turf they all stood on right now.

It was enough to set Josephine in a shitty mood for the whole week.

This detail, though, was soon forgotten as she followed along on the heels of the crew, headed up the stairs to the mansion, and to the enormous, oak front doors. Josephine had to admit that, if she had been a ghost, this mansion would be a pretty terrific place to hang out.

From the looks on the faces of the three mediums—but Alburton's especially—she saw that she was not alone in this assumption.

They passed through the rooms with great speed, at such a speed that Josephine was sure that the director, who was leading them along, had memorised a floor plan of the mansion. She guessed that there was really no time to waste. They needed to get everything set up before night rolled in. They needed to be ready for whatever might be coming.

If anything was coming at all.

The director barked orders at them all, reading them each off abridged instructions for how they should each find their bedrooms in the mansion.

Josephine hardly caught the instructions, but thought that she had caught enough so as not to need to ask for the director to repeat himself. She didn't want to make herself the centre of attention. She wanted to merely slip into the shadows, to allow them to see her as part of the scenery.

The bedroom that she had been assigned had a thin layer of dust covering just about everything. Whenever Josephine breathed in, the dust caught at the back of her throat, and it seemed to render the aftertaste of banana in her mouth sour, almost *rotten*.

As she moved about the bedroom, she caught a draught sneaking in around the neck of her shirt, and she heard herself give a gasp.

It took her the best part of a few seconds to gather herself back together, to tell herself, once again, that there was *no such thing* as ghosts, and, strangely enough, it seemed to do the trick.

Her bed was a four-poster and it had a netted curtain which hung down on all sides. The linen, she saw when she brushed her fingertips along it, was clean and had been recently put there. She wondered if it was the caretaker himself who had done it, or if, in just like all the ghost tales she'd read in her childhood, the caretaker's wife had been charged with the housekeeping duties.

Josephine padded over to the shuttered window, undid the unoiled latch, and then spread the shutters wide, opening them back towards herself. Despite the chill it was kicking up outside, she opened the windows.

This was one of those places that almost *demanded* a breath of life.

To make it seem more a mansion and less a mausoleum.

That done, and her rucksack set at the foot of the bed, Josephine checked out the bathroom adjoining.

Black-and-white tiles covered the walls and floors, and one of those old-style bathtubs—the kind with metal animal paws for feet—stood ready. It had a pair of rusty stains on the yellowing porcelain beneath each of the taps. She saw that there was no shower attachment, so it seemed like she would have to spend this week taking baths.

A minor annoyance.

Everything looked clean about the bathroom, if not—just a touch—over-used.

But was that a bad thing in a place like this?

She supposed it was a *very good thing* for the mediums since they made their bread by speaking to ghosties . . . and if the rooms here, at one point in the past, had been bustling with activity then it meant, by extension, that surely some people had *died* here.

And with that morbid thought on her mind, Josephine headed back to the bed, and dug through her rucksack.

3

JOSEPHINE SPREAD OUT all the pieces of kit which he client had provided her.

She had a pair of small microphones—two of them so that, if one of them was defective, or got broken, she would have a backup.

Then there was the small audio recorder which the microphone plugged into.

A pinhole camera which she was supposed to wear at all times.

And then, finally, the notebook where she was supposed to write up her thoughts after the end of each day . . . or *night* she supposed, according to the mediums' domain.

She had another notebook with her, of course, but it was only a prop.

Something to pull out if she needed to prove her journalistic credentials at any point.

She had nothing else along with her—and her client had assured her that this was all the proof that he would require, if she could just—maybe—get one of the mediums on tape saying something incriminating, preferably while looking direct into the pinhole camera, then she would've been a resounding success.

As Josephine sat there, alone in her room, the contents of her rucksack all yanked out and left on her bed, she plugged one of the microphones into the audio recorder and then placed it in the pocket of her fleece.

The pinhole camera she disguised as a button at the breast pocket of the fleece, just as she had planned.

And with that, all her tools equipped, she waited sitting on the edge of the bed, and thought about nothing really at all.

4

I T HAD JUST GONE eight o'clock in the evening when Alburton knocked on her bedroom door. With that same, slick —*greasy*—grin of his, he told her that dinner 'was served.'

She followed the babble of voices along the corridors, and she was surprised to hear so much laughter among the chatter. Strange considering what they had come here, to this mansion, to *supposedly* do.

She stepped in over the threshold to the hall where the voices seemed to be emanating from and she was immediately struck by the grandness of the room. The ceiling was towering and it had those wooden beams high above which always put Josephine in mind of a whale's bone structure. It smelled of polish in here, and the air felt lighter, like somebody thought to throw open the windows once in a while to guard against damp. It felt almost like Josephine had taken a step inside by comparison with her own bedroom.

The whole team sat down on a long, wooden bench which looked like it had been pilfered from a chapel, perhaps hidden within the many rooms of the mansion. Their food stood before them, steaming away on plastic plates, resting on a long wooden table.

The whole image set Josephine in mind of a medieval banquet hall.

Dinner, it turned out, consisted of tinned beans on buttered toast.

Josephine supposed that she should've been glad that somebody had thought to bring along a toaster at all.

During the course of the meal, she established that just about everybody, or everybody who *commented*, was a vegetarian—or maybe they were vegan, though she couldn't really tell the difference. And when the line of questioning eventually rolled around to Josephine, she thought a second about lying and then decided that, since she was lying about so much else, it was probably better to play this particular enquiry with a straight bat.

"No," Josephine said, "I'm a meat-eater."

There was a lingering silence following *that* comment.

"Well," the director said, "Guess there's still time to come around."

An uncomfortable round of laughter followed this, though Josephine struggled to see what was funny about it. Maybe it was that famous psychic humour she'd heard about . . . or the lack of it . . .

When they finished up dinner, the team whirred into action right away.

The soundman, with his long boom mike, and the cameraman, with his—surely-too-small-for-TV—camera, conferred over in one of the corners of the hall.

The director was speaking with the three mediums.

The driver was nowhere to be seen and Josephine wondered if he'd decided to sleep out in his van rather than in this creepy mansion.

Sensible guy.

Just do as much as they're *paying* you to do.

Which was as much as what Josephine intended to do for her client.

Since Josephine really didn't know where she should stand: with the mediums or the TV crew, she decided to keep herself on the fringes, to simply stand back and allow her camera and mike to pick up whatever they would.

As she stood there, she felt a tightness in her chest, a slight apprehension. It was funny, back when she'd been having dinner with her client, back when he was pitching her the job, he had gone on a sceptical rampage which had encompassed just about everything: from religion, to belief systems in general, to the eventual subject, the 'spirit world' . . . he had made the inverted commas with his fingers when he had said that particular phrase out loud.

Although Josephine had found herself agreeing to his sentiments, she couldn't say that she had particularly enjoyed his manner of delivery. The way he was so confrontational, treating *those people* like they were some sort of an evil entity on their own, and, in a way which Josephine found ironic, displaying that same religious fervour present in those that he so openly reviled.

But Josephine had said nothing, of course, she needed the money.

And the half payment that he had given her had helped her to pay off around half of the debts she'd accumulated in her private investigation business. She had had to really go out on a limb to have her creditors wait for the rest of the payment, and she wouldn't be at all surprised, on returning to her modest office, to discover a pair of heavies waiting there, each holding a cricket bat, each percussively patting theirs against their respective palms.

When she got the job done, she would be back in the black.

Back to showing everyone that she *could* make a success of herself.

No matter how much they all wanted her to fail.

"Okay then!" Alburton said, clapping his hands together. "Let's get going."

It was only now that Josephine realised, with a sense of creeping dread, that Alburton was in charge here. That, though the director was obviously in *technical* charge, Alburton was the one who was truly calling the shots.

There was something she really didn't like . . . didn't *trust* . . . about Alburton.

And she made a note to stay on her guard.

As the team moved out, with the director at the head of the group, Alburton hung back. He met Josephine's eye, gave her a smile, and then said, "Ready to go ghost hunting, then?"

JOSEPHINE WAS TAKEN ABACK by the darkness. Stupidly, she hadn't thought to bring a torch with her. She had naively assumed that, since they were going to be staying in a house, there would be electric lights to guide them. She had never really considered that the mediums would want to switch off the lights . . . perhaps she should've been paying more attention when she'd watched those *Mediums of the Midnight Mansion* shows.

The show that she might find herself appearing on now inadvertently.

As they had entered the darkness, Josephine had made a point of sticking near the back of the group. Her logic was simple, she didn't want to be anywhere near Alburton in the pitch-black. And not just because he seemed like a creep. But there was *something else* . . . something else that she *felt* clinging to him.

With a slight smirk in the darkness that nobody else could see, she wondered just what her client would've made of *that* thought.

About her being 'taken in' by a 'con artist.'

They continued on into the darkness, stopping about every ten or so paces for the mediums to close ranks, to reach their hands about themselves. One of them liked to hum lightly under her breath, while the other just stood stony still in the darkness, and as Josephine could make out from the others' torchlight, with his eyes wide open and shining like glass. Alburton, though, as far as Josephine could tell, did nothing in particular. To her—admittedly untrained—eye, he seemed to simply stand at the front of the group whenever they stopped and grin widely.

They'd been going for about three hours before she heard the first excited *peep* from one of the mediums: the one who liked to close her eyes hum.

"Here," the medium said. "Here."

Josephine felt a tingle run up her spine. A chill pass through her blood. She had the odd urge to run away, to escape. But, at the same time, her sceptical self knew that she was just being stupid, that she was being one of those who her client would've referred to as an 'enabler,' those who actually legitimised the cons that these mediums tried to pull on people.

She held still.

Remembered the pinhole camera, and the mike she had running in her pocket.

But the cameras were still around her.

She knew that the most likely way she would get her job done would be if she managed to get one of the mediums alone—one-on-one. They weren't likely to give away anything that her client could use if the cameras were still rolling.

Right then, with that thought on her mind, she saw Alburton's grinning face, the smile pinning back the corners of his mouth. Gently, he reached forwards and laid a hand on the shoulder of the female medium. "Come on," he said. "Nothing to see here, I don't think."

And then, clearly, with no explanation, he gave the director a wink and led the group on.

It was at that moment that Josephine realised that her best chance of gathering evidence against these mediums was to get Alburton alone. To get him to speak frankly.

With no cameras.

Except her own.

6

THEY STOPPED another three times at varying places in the mansion, and Josephine took care to study Alburton each time that they did. She wanted to check him for more clues. Wanted to see him give himself away to her—and to her pinhole camera—another time.

But he seemed to become a little more serious about his work, that smile of his only came up whenever they'd stopped for several moments and he—because it was *always* him—had decided that there was nothing to see there.

Still, that didn't shake Josephine's confidence any that Alburton was her best bet at getting the job done.

After they'd been walking for what seemed like hours and hours, and when Josephine checked her watch she saw that it had just gone two o'clock in the morning, Alburton brought an abrupt end to the expedition.

Josephine was glad.

The soles of her feet were sore.

Her head was a little dizzy from walking so long through the near darkness.

And, on the contrary, rather than making her feel afraid to climb into bed, all this walking about the mansion in the dead of night had actually made her feel better about things. There was nothing to be afraid of that she could see here.

The only real—*tangible*—thing to be afraid of was Alburton.

As they headed back down to the hall where they had eaten dinner, Josephine felt a jump of confidence, some sort of an internal mechanism, what she had always believed to be the *talent* she housed for being a private investigator. And it told her now that this was the perfect time to begin her interrogation of Alburton.

As the TV crew packed their gear away—though under instructions from the director to keep their camera and boom mike in a state so that they were ready 'if anything should go bump in the night'—Josephine wished the other mediums good night, while simultaneously managing to collar Alburton under the pretence of doing an interview.

With a gentle smile, Alburton gladly accepted, and they took a seat opposite one another on the wooden bench where they'd eaten dinner.

"So," Alburton said, "remind me of the format this piece will take."

Josephine met his sapphire eyes, those eyes which, she supposed, had been quite the charmers in his young manhood. Now, though, they had more of an air of distrust. She could see just where all the scepticism surrounding him and other psychics sprang from looking into *those* eyes.

Josephine picked up her well-prepared patter. "The magazine wants me to run a blow-by-blow, hour-by-hour rundown of how the show is put together. So"—she paused for a second to dig into her pocket for the notepad she kept there and then to slap it down on the table—"what I've got here," she said, pointing out the observations she'd already written up, "is notes on what things have happened, the *order* they've happened, you know, stuff like that."

Alburton stuck out his lower lip and half turned his head as he attempted to read Josephine's upside-down notes. He soon tired of trying to decipher her scrawl. Josephine had taken special care to make her writing as obscure as possible, and that really hadn't been too tough of a task since she'd been writing in near darkness.

Alburton rested back on the bench. He laid his hands on the table before him. Laid them flat against the surface, and then, with a slight smile, he said, "Would you like me to give you a reading?"

"'A reading?'" Josephine repeated, not thinking clearly.

Alburton gave a gentle smile. "Yes, I can tell just what's in store for you this week." He paused for a second. "Only if you'd *like* me to, of course."

Josephine thought over the offer. She tried to think things through from her position, from the journalist that she was supposed to be. Would somebody authentic, in her position, decide for or against this? Would they be intimidated by the mansion's negative 'energy?'

Or would they simply leap at the opportunity to have such a *prestigious* psychic pay them so much attention?

In the end, and maybe Josephine was thinking things through more from her client's perspective—she *was* on his payroll, after all —she went with the latter.

And, just like that, she found herself holding hands with Alburton.

Worse, as she noticed, right as their hands touched, the director and his two crew members were leaving the hall, wishing them both a good night.

She thought about the can of pepper spray she had smuggled into the bottom of her rucksack. 'If in doubt, pull it out,' that was what she'd learned at the campus safety talk back at university, and she guessed that it would serve her just as well in the real world.

For the first time that night—or early morning, as it had just gone three a.m.—Alburton closed his eyes and his smile dissolved from his lips. As he touched her hands, Josephine was certain that she could feel a low-level hum passing through her.

She wondered if it was just her imagination.

Or if it was really happening.

They sat like that for what felt like about a minute, and then, in a low, steady voice, Alburton said, "I see darkness."

Josephine risked rolling her eyes, seeing as Alburton had his eyes shut.

This really did bring her back to the surface, made her see her client's point of view.

Whenever she had gone to a psychic reading before, she had always found them just about as relevant as a newspaper horoscope.

"Darkness and pain," Alburton added, screwing up his expression, his eyes still closed.

Josephine was tempted to let out a sigh. She busied herself looking about the hall. Taking in the several paintings which hung down from the walls, but which were cover in white sheets, apparently to keep the dust off them.

Alburton squeezed her hands.

And he kept squeezing.

Till Josephine felt pain.

When it became too much, she couldn't stop herself letting out a little *yelp*.

This brought Alburton back round. He released her from his grip and blinked several times, apparently bringing the physical world back into focus after having lost himself to the spiritual one. He gradually turned his attention back onto her, and then said, in a slow, even voice, and without a trace of a smile, "You don't belong here, do you?"

7

JOSEPHINE FELT a prickling sensation within her chest. She stared back into his sapphire eyes. Into those light-blue shades, that colour which brought into mind the shallows of a tropical sea. "What?" she said, her voice feeling tight, and her throat impossibly dry.

Alburton continued to regard her, his expression tight, his lips now pressed hard together so much so that it squeezed all the blood from them. He breathed in deeply and his shoulders rose up, made him seem much taller than he actually was.

For the first time since she'd come to the mansion, Josephine felt palpably afraid.

She wanted to get out *right now*.

Sure, she would have the bills to worry about, the creditors, and she would no doubt have to trek all those miles back to the main road and then try to hitch a lift.

But she would work it all out.

If she could just get out of here *now*.

They sat like that, regarding one another, for a long few moments, and then, as if somebody had flicked a switch, Alburton cracked a smile, and then bashed the table with his palm. He chuckled. "Oh, come on!" he said. "I think we can speak frankly—can't we? I mean, we're on the same side."

Josephine felt herself twitching all over. Her muscles were bundled up so tight that it felt like they might break through her skin at any second. When she breathed in, the air was sharp with the stench of polish. She could taste blood in her mouth. Her heart thumped loud, *percussive* thuds in her ears.

Alburton leaned across the table and he gave her a gentle slap on the shoulder. "I thought as much when I first saw you—didn't think that you were as gullible as the others we've got here."

He jerked his thumb off in the direction the director and his crew had headed out, though Josephine was fairly certain he was referring to the other two mediums rather than the TV crew.

Feeling the full daze of Alburton's smile on her now, and feeling more and more unnerved by the second, feeling like she was only clinging to her disguise by a thread, she tried her best to mimic him. To give him at least a flimsy smile.

She managed it.

But only just.

Alburton gave a yawn, which he barely stifled with the back of his hand, and then he rose to his feet. "Come on," he said. "Think it's time for bed."

Josephine's mind moved onto other matters in that second. Her mind turned, once more, to the pepper spray concealed in her rucksack.

However, it seemed, if Alburton did in fact have any intentions involving her, that tonight—at the very least—he simply didn't have the energy.

Like the gentleman she was sure he believed himself to be, Alburton led her to her bedroom door and then wished her goodnight with a slight peck on the cheek.

Only when Josephine got her bedroom door shut behind her, and listened to the sound of Alburton's footsteps disappearing off along the hallway—his own bedroom door open and then slap shut —could she allow herself to relax her muscles.

She stayed standing for another couple of minutes, listening out for anything at all, any sign of a returning threat. But, it seemed, she had got away with it for now.

And, as she took a few steps into her bedroom, she suddenly remembered the mike she'd had in her pocket throughout their conversation—the pinhole camera—and she allowed herself a smile.

She got the day's activities all written out in her authentic notebook, along with her observations about Alburton, that he seemed to have been not only hinting at a conspiracy within the society of mediums, but also the media which accompanied it.

This kind of evidence, for her client, would be nothing less than dynamite, she was sure.

As she slipped beneath the covers of her bed, checking to see that the time had now gone four in the morning, she allowed herself a slight sense of satisfaction at a good night's work.

She had managed to gain Alburton's trust.

And he, she was sure, would be the key to her report.

It was only when Josephine was slipping away to sleep that she forced herself back around. She slipped the covers off herself and padded over to her rucksack, resting upright on a chair. She pawed through it and uncovered the pepper spray.

When she returned to bed, pulled the covers back over herself, she nestled the pepper spray beneath her pillow. Within reach of a snatching hand if she needed it.

8

JOSEPHINE SLEPT for a long time, and when she woke, she saw that it had gone midday.

As she rose from her bed, she had that pleasant—and *deep* —feeling that she'd got herself a terrific night's sleep. Perhaps it was something about the bed, how she could simply sink into it and drift away. Maybe it had to do with the mansion's quiet surroundings and how there wasn't so much as a twittering bird to wake her up.

Though she felt like she had been sleeping away while everyone was busy, she was pleasantly surprised to find that the mansion was totally deserted.

Nobody else was up and about yet.

Breakfast, though, she saw, was already set up and waiting for her.

A single packet of cereal which sat beside a pile of bowls.

Some fogged-up, not-totally-clean cutlery lying—and sparkling in the sunlight—alongside.

Josephine sat and crunched her way through the sugary cereal. She gave the milk a try too, and found it creamy and rich. She wondered if it had been sourced from one of the many farms which surrounded the mansion. She almost never saw milk in a glass bottle these days.

It was strange to think that what had once been ordinary in her youth was now, in the present, somewhat *quaint*.

Once Josephine had eaten, she padded through the still-deserted mansion, marvelling at how deeply mediums could really sleep. Only when she returned to her bedroom did she find herself speculating all those many things she'd seen in horror films. Where the protagonist would wake up and find everybody gone. That everything had been a dream. Nothing more than an illusion. But, unlike *those* protagonists, Josephine had the proof.

Just to assure herself, though she was careful to point out—within her own mind—that she was just doing it to test that everything had recorded fine, she listened back to a few minutes from the audio recording from the night before.

The conversation with herself and Alburton.

Yep, the voices, at least, were real.

Unless she had a whole bunch of auditory hallucinations going on too . . .

It was early evening before Josephine heard any voices in the corridor outside her bedroom. When she emerged, she saw that it was Alburton and one of the psychics—the *male* psychic. They were speaking in hushed tones, but they both smiled widely at Josephine when she emerged from her bedroom.

Alburton approached her. "So," he said, "all set for another night's hunting?"

9

S LOWLY, Josephine found herself seeping into the routine of the psychics.

Night after night, she found herself getting used to losing the second half of the morning, and then taking full advantage of the evenings.

Earlier on, when she'd first struck up her PI business, she'd got an assignment which had required her to stake out a house during the night. It was then that she had really wondered how on *Earth* anybody could actually go through with a nightshift regularly.

She would sleep most of the day and wake up right when the sun was going down.

It was depressing without measure.

Now, though, this was different.

She found herself wondering whether the mansion might've been having a calming—*healing*—effect on her.

Just listen to her now, her client really would have given her a tongue-lashing . . .

She kept her eye fixed on all the psychics as they went about their work. And she watched on as things seemed to get more serious. As Alburton stopped appearing so flippant, how he seemed to increase in seriousness. Got himself interested in any little detail.

Josephine wondered—sceptically—whether this might be because he had a deadline that he was up against. That he knew that he needed to get this programme turned in by the end of the week and the TV crew needed the footage. But she tried to stay neutral, attempted to keep herself from making any judgements. Her role here was simply to *observe* after all.

One night, after a good night's 'hunting,' she managed to corner the other two psychics and—miracle of all miracles—without having Alburton breathing down their necks.

It was similar to the scene before, when she had managed to corner Alburton in the hall, only this time they were completely and totally alone. The TV crew had already packed up their gear and headed off to bed. Tonight they had called off the hunt a little earlier because they'd had some good 'contact,' which, to Josephine, had mainly seemed to constitute one of the three mediums—usually the younger two members—coming to a sudden halt, letting out a piercing scream and then running away.

Josephine hadn't stuck around, though, she hadn't been in the mood to confirm her theory.

But she sat here, now, with the pair of mediums.

With the man and the woman.

It had been hard for her to get the two of them alone. She had had to shake off Alburton—like a concerned parent constantly buzzing around them.

And now, as she stared back at the psychics, the pair of them impossibly serious, Josephine scribbled down everything that they dished up for her.

There was nothing dynamite in what they said. It was more about the things that seemed to be implied about the edges. Things which Josephine could pick up on impulse.

But which, from her client's perspective, would be no good for use as evidence.

He only wanted 'concrete' findings.

After she'd got done with the interview, only really having a pair of fairly dull life stories which, if she *had* been working for the magazine she'd made out she had, knew would only make a pair of one-sentence sidebars to the main article. At best.

And it was with that that she headed for her bedroom, knowing, in the morning, they would all be leaving the mansion. That Josephine would be headed home with just what she'd got. Though it seemed like she'd got nothing at all here, with all her contact with Alburton, she got the feeling that, since her camera had been rolling the entire time—her audio recorder too—it really wasn't all that bad . . . she would wait to see what her client said about the matter, whether or not he considered her job here a failure or a success.

And so, if it wasn't with optimism that she shifted into her bedroom, it was at least with relief—relief that this would all be over in the morning.

It was only when she pulled the sheets over her and lay on her back in bed that she heard the gentle footsteps out in the corridor.

10

JOSEPHINE CLUNG TIGHT to the hem of her blanket—quite unable to shift herself.

She was exhausted.

When she peeked through the darkness, to the chest of drawers across from her, she realised that she'd simply peeled off all her gear: the audio recorder, the camera, and left them out on the top. Anybody that walked in here would see them right away.

But why would anybody walk into her bedroom in the middle of the night?

She observed the doorknob to her bedroom twist a little.

Her blood ran cold.

She wondered if she was imagining things.

And yet she believed her eyes.

The door opened quietly, shifting away to reveal an even more profound darkness.

Josephine held still in bed, as if nobody would notice her lying there if only she forced herself not to move.

Three figures entered her bedroom.

For some reason, she expected them to go through her chest of drawers, to go through her things, but they didn't. They all stood still and they stared at her through the mounted-up blackness.

It was strange, Josephine caught the impression that this was some sort of a dark performance, as if, beyond there, beyond the darkness, there was a hushed audience waiting with the same bated breath she held.

Only when one of the figures spoke did Josephine put all of the pieces together. "Josephine?"

It was Alburton.

His voice was steady—mundane, even—and it sounded like he

was a little regretful that he couldn't be tucked up in bed, drifting off to sleep, right now.

Josephine didn't reply.

But that didn't seem to bother Alburton

"We know who you are, Josephine," he said. "We know who you *really* are."

Josephine held still. She reached under her pillow for the can of pepper spray.

But it was gone.

She scrabbled about for it briefly, but still couldn't locate it.

Her muscles all pulled tight.

"You must understand," Alburton continued, "that there's such a thing as an omertà—things which, quite simply, cannot be allowed to escape from a certain circle of trust. You surely must understand that."

Josephine couldn't speak. She felt like the three of them, standing there in the darkness, pinned her down with their gaze. And, when she looked closely, she realised that there were only two figures now. She glanced about herself frantically, wanted to run.

And yet she knew that they still blocked the door.

It was only when Josephine felt a sharp, burning sensation in her left arm that she thought to look to her left. To see the figure there. Injecting something into her.

As the figure retreated from her side, joined the other three figures, she felt her limbs all go floppy, her heart making a squeezing effort to keep pumping. When she spoke, it was like somebody held a pillow over her mouth, though she could quite plainly see all three of the figures standing up there, before her, motionless.

"What . . . will you . . ."

Though she couldn't complete her sentence, it seemed to be enough for Alburton to generate a response. "We'll do with you like we did all the others—bury you alive, out the back of the mansion."

And with that thought, and the thought that she had failed her client, Josephine felt herself slipping back, down into her bed, and getting away from them all.

Forever.

RAMBLER

1

A CRISP WIND blew round the collar of Peter's fleece. He zipped it up to his chin and snuggled his nose below the line of the material. Clouds were rolling over the hills, plunging down like frothed up waves. He sighed internally at the dirge this day had descended into—no trace of the bright September sunshine that had woken him that morning.

Raindrops spotted the gravel path and the smell of damp earth clung to Peter's nostrils. He was going to have to set up camp before the weather came in. He didn't fancy pitching a tent with a gale on his back and rain soaking everything.

He pulled a waterproof from his backpack and thrust it down over his head, pulling up the hood and tightening the drawstring, so as to cover his whole face apart from his eyes and the bridge of his nose.

The scrape of boots over stones carried on the wind and a pair of fellow walkers appeared from over the lip of the hill ahead. They seemed no more than shadows in the dim daylight, a foggy mirage. A black dog trotted between them, its nose to the track, haunches trembling and tail twitching along behind it.

A gust of wind whistled in from Peter's side and he shivered, thinking of his warm room at the pub, The Ditcher's Arms, where he had stayed the night before—the baked beef pie with steaming gravy and the pleasantly warm ale to top it off. If he just turned back he could put up for another night. He was sure that no one would've taken the room. This place was pretty out of the way. In fact, he was quite surprised to see this pair of walkers here. Then again, he supposed it impossible to keep this area a secret forever, what with its ghostly-grey hills, ethereal long grasses and crystalline streams.

The dog padded up to him, tongue lolling out of the corner of its mouth, beady black eyes peering up at him. It sniffed round his kneecaps and then ankles, before tilting its head up.

Peter put his weather-induced misery to one side and crouched down to stroke the dog's head. His fur felt warm to the touch. He scratched the area behind its ears and held its head in his hands. He had had a dog when he'd been much younger—six or seven. He'd been called Muss, short for Diotimus, the Greek philosopher—his father was a philosophy academic, so he often had to suffer things like that.

He looked the dog straight in the eye and said, "You're just like Muss, aren't you?"

The dog's owners trod closer, like a pair of crime scene investigators with their anoraks covering every patch of skin save their eyes and noses. The man was thin and tall, and walked with a wide gait. The woman, too, was tall, but a little plumper. She had wide hips. They stopped when they reached him, and the man said, "Fancy you setting off out here in this weather, must be half mad."

The woman elbowed the man—presumably her husband—in the ribs. "Don't be rude, Gerald." She looked Peter up and down. "He has got a point, though, weather's really whipping up, especially up ahead, through the pass."

Peter gave the dog a parting pat and rose. "It's all right, I'm planning on camping out. Thinking that I'll set up somewhere near by and see if it doesn't clear up later on."

"Out here for the weekend, then?"

"That's right."

"What, just rambling along?"

"Yeah."

"Shame about the weather."

"Yeah."

She puckered her lips. "You look quite young, about my daughter's age."

"Is that right?" Peter said, growing increasingly aware that the chill was picking up and the rain was beginning to come down in sheets, to patter against the watertight fabric of his hood.

"She would never come out here, though, not alone."

"Would she not?"

The woman glanced to her husband. "To tell the truth, neither would either of us."

"Why's that then?"

"Haven't you heard?"

"Heard what?"

"There's been people going missing round here."

Bracing himself for a set of tall tales, Peter looked round. He located the dog off amongst some bracken, sniffing about in some rabbit holes, apparently unaffected by the now driving rain.

"Yeah," the woman said, "there's this girl, right, came out here camping after breaking up with her boyfriend, or something. Well, down in The Ditcher's Arms they were keeping an eye out—as they always do—and when she never returned they contacted the police." The woman sniffled, within her hood. "Found her tent out there"—she pointed off vaguely, back down the path, toward the pass—"no trace of her, though. She was gone."

"What do you mean 'just gone?'"

"Never found the body."

"How horrible."

"Had to bring all her stuff back up the trail, looked round for months, but never found anything."

Now feeling decidedly stone-cold about this whole weekend plan, he considered whether he might be better advised to turn round, get back to The Ditcher's and snuggle down into his warm bed, crack on with his eight-hundred page, nineteenth century novel —relishing the mingling of solitude with long dead words.

The woman rubbed her hands together and leant into her husband's chest for warmth. "Then there was that man, bit older if

I remember, he camped off down the pass. That one was different, though. None of his stuff was even found. Just a couple of forgotten pegs, where he'd pitched his tent."

"Suicides, though?" Peter said.

"Most likely. Course they never could come to an official verdict, not yet, anyway, with them being so soon gone missing, not without finding the bodies, but that's the general consensus, down The Ditcher's, anyway."

The husband stared over his wife's head at Peter. "What's got into you coming here, then?"

Peter eyed the dog as it returned from the bracken and coiled itself round his shins, shuddering and panting. He reached down and lost his fingertips in its thick fur. "Ah, thought I could just do with a break, that's all, end of year exams and all that. Got a couple of weekends free before I start into working full-time at my summer job." He summoned a smile onto his numb lips. "All being well I should get out of uni pretty much debt-free."

The man eyeballed him, keeping him fixed in his glare. "That's all, then, is it?"

"Yeah."

The man continued to stare. "How come you're out here all alone, then?"

Peter realised the man was connecting the dots, considering the two cases the woman had outlined, the suicides, he believed that he had some ulterior motive for coming out here, that he wasn't being completely sincere with the couple. But, then again, them being strangers and all, why should he be?

Peter straightened out his expression, feeling a chill grow from within his chest. "Don't need anyone else. I like to be alone, that's all."

The man kept up his eye contact, and the moan of the wind and the splatter of the rain against their coats were the only sounds for several seconds.

The woman snorted a laugh then jabbed her husband in the ribs again. "Gerald, don't be such a fiend, I'm sure he'll be fine out here —he looks a responsible lad to me." She glanced back at Peter. "Gerald's just concerned, that's all. You know, with this weather we're having. He doesn't want to think about you out here all alone." She produced a lead from within the pocket of her anorak, and stooped down to attach it to the dog's collar. "If you'd like you can walk back with us. Our car's parked a little down the road, off into onc of the hedges. Save you the walk down to The Ditcher's?"

Peter recalled the car, a sludge-green estate with the mud splashed up its sides, several scratches on the driver's side where it appeared to have had a scrape with another car, coming round a corner—common to lots of cars round here, an occupational hazard of the narrow lanes with bushy grass verges obscuring the view.

He considered the offer. It was kind of the woman and he saw just where she was coming from. Like she'd said, she had a kid his age, and was probably looking out for him. That happened some-times with older women when they saw him alone—he always reminded them of someone.

Then he remembered why he'd come here, and he shook his head solemnly. "Thanks, anyway."

"You sure, love?" the woman said.

"Yeah."

She sighed. "All right, then." She rolled her shoulders and wrapped her arm round her husband. "We'd better be off, otherwise there'll be three blocks of ice here." She nodded to the dog. "Eric'll have to go off and find help."

"Wouldn't want that," Peter said.

As the couple passed by, Peter kept his eyes to the path, nodding to them without looking up. He was sure that the husband continued to stare at him. After they'd gone, he watched them walk away from him—the dog skittering about at their heels.

He allowed himself to exhale. His chest felt tight following the conversation—standing round in the cold. He gripped his backpack straps tight and proceeded along the path.

H IS TEARS took him by surprise. The rain now was so steady that, at first, he wasn't sure where his tears ended and the raindrops began. He strode on, feeling his throat well with phlegm and his cheeks chill in the harsh wind. He felt angry with those two walkers—the man and wife—although there was no way that they could've known. They didn't realise how insensitive they had acted. He told himself that if he had just thought to mention his connection to those missing ramblers then they might've changed their tone. But then, he was sure, they would've insisted on his returning with them, going back to The Ditcher's Arms, and he never would've got the closure he sought.

Rain collected onto the end of his nose and dripped down, sending a shudder across his skin. A dull tingle at the rim of his skull suggested the onset of a migraine. The path overflowed with water, the stream had burst its banks and surged over the dirt. The thick tread of his boots sucked against the sodden surface. He traipsed onward.

He came upon the pass about twenty minutes later. He stopped, so wet that he no longer noticed the rain, and scrutinised the scenery, as if it *itself* might be the culprit for the horrors which plagued him.

"Yes," he had wanted to say to the woman, "I heard all about the girl. That *girl* had a name. She was called Rebecca. She was my girlfriend. In fact she was more than that, she was my *fiancée*."

His tears snaked down his cheeks and mingled with the rainwater which seeped down his collar, wetting his chest and the backs of his shoulders. He crunched his teeth together and looked down into the valley several metres below, and he examined the camping ground—the last known location of Rebecca, where they'd found her possessions.

Her face was already fading from his mind. It was funny how that happened. Of course he had hundreds of photos on his computer, but he could never bring himself to look at them—or delete them. He had seen her almost every day, ever since they'd met on one of the first days of university, waiting to register in bulk at their local doctor's office. It had been a quirk of surnames, just the fact that his surname: Tankard, had preceded hers, Tanner. The nurse had ordered them in the waiting room—a real battle-axe—insisted that they all be in correct order, because far be it from the doctor to have to call out their names individually when the time came.

The upshot of the whole affair was that he, a computer science student, had sat next to Rebecca, who was studying political history. Never, aside from a chance meeting in the Students' Union—which Peter had an almost religious aversion to—or the library, which Peter had no reason to visit, considering that he had already bought all the course books he needed, would they have had reason to meet.

Whatever Casanova was, Peter had been the opposite. Like the typical computer science student he had been impossibly awkward sitting there in his plastic seat, squirming away because there was a *girl* beside him. Predictably, it had been Rebecca who had fired up the conversation. She had complimented him on his shoes, said that they looked 'cool.'

Sweating all over and considering what kind of an impact this meeting might have on his impending blood pressure reading, Peter did his best to explain that he had had his shoes for a long time that, actually, they were his father's and he had taken to using them since they fit him fine.

Something about what he'd said had been funny because she'd given him a chirrupy laugh, then they'd sat silently for a long time, and Peter might've just left things there, never have spoken to her again, returned to the darkened confines of his room, stooped over his fluorescent computer monitor, scribing line after line of code.

And then, sidelong, he'd got a proper look at her. He'd seen her thin blond hair and her light-blue eyes, her skinny frame and almost non-existent breasts, her faintly freckled cheeks, her pasty skin. She tapped through her phone, seemingly unaware of him watching.

He must've sounded like an idiot, the oldest trick in the book, asking her if she'd like to go for a drink later. He still remembered those various phases of her expressions, how she'd moved from confusion, that he was speaking to her at all, continuing a conversation he'd seemed so set on ending, then onto surprise, that he was asking this out of the blue, and then onto acceptance, a wry smile pinning back the corners of her mouth.

Then his turn with the doctor had come up and he'd left her behind.

He stared down into the valley, through the veils of rain, trying to work out where she might've pitched her tent, the thoughts and feelings that must've streamed through her mind as she did so. But he failed, again. Throughout their relationship, and he realised it applied to just about all his relationships, not just romantic ones—or should be *the* romantic one—he found it almost impossible to second guess what people were thinking. They were a mass of snaking wires and programs to him, impossibly complex and opaque. He supposed he got it from his father. He had always noted how, at dinner, his mother would pick through some topic of conversation while his father remained whirling away in his own world—no doubt breaking some facet or other of reality, pinning it down for philosophical examination, like a butterfly collector and his cork board. Forever bemused.

Feeling the water soak into the toe and heel of his socks, Peter headed on along the slippery pass and down into the valley.

3

PETER THOUGHT he would never get the tent up. Every time he unfurled the canvas it would flap, unruly in the wind. To be honest, he had hardly done much camping in his life—not for several years. Before he'd left home, he'd practised putting up his tent in the garage, waiting till his parents had gone off to do the weekly shop so as not to raise suspicion. Doing it out here, in the open, was completely different, though. He had had no wind or rain to contend with in the draughty, but dry garage.

The inside was sodden by the time he crawled inside, leaving his boots at the entrance, and he was glad for his thermos, which the lady back at The Ditcher's Arms had filled with hot coffee that morning. He poured it out into the plastic lid-cum-mug and watched the steam curl up into the air.

The rain rapped against the canvas and, despite the dampness, he felt himself warming from the inside, thanks to the coffee. If this rain didn't let up, if the sun didn't break through the clouds this afternoon and dry out his equipment he would have reason to worry about the night ahead. The coffee would've gone cold by then and his wet clothes would become his death blanket.

He thought about how he felt, being here, where she had slept. He had never believed in ghosts or anything supernatural—never had reason to—but it was impossible to deny the sense of anticipation circulating through him. Why else had he come here if he wasn't looking for some trace, some remainder of Rebecca?

He was a realist. He had long given up hope that she might be alive. It just didn't happen that way. People didn't simply disappear and then reappear, not when they went off into the woods. But, still, he hoped to find something here. Perhaps she might've left behind some item of clothing, a scrunchie half trampled into the ground or a stray earring—perhaps one of those silver ones he'd given her for her birthday earlier this year.

More than anything else he just wanted to know why. Why had she done this? Had she been unhappy? Why had she never confided in him, told him how she felt? The day before the exam period started she had simply disappeared, only to turn up here when the lady who ran The Ditcher's had phoned the police on recognising her appearance from the descriptions being bandied about. And then she'd just gone, slipped off the face of the Earth. Or had she? He flexed his mind back before that, to meeting Darren Tanner, Rebecca's father.

Strange that their first meeting should be in their mutual search for his daughter, Peter's girlfriend. Darren had obviously been driving himself spare wondering what had happened to Rebecca. He had talked to some of the girls who lived with Rebecca and got the story that Peter had been her boyfriend, and so he'd come knocking, quizzing him for any details. He left in frustration when Peter told him that he had no idea, but not before issuing Peter a warning—that if Peter ended up being implicated in any way with Rebecca's disappearance, he would kill him.

After he'd gone, Peter remembered perching on the edge of his bed, knees hunched up to his chest, shivering, wondering whether in some way he might be 'implicated.' He wondered whether he had said something to set her off or if he could've acted any different. In the end he was resigned to sitting and waiting for news. And then Darren, too, had gone missing. That was when Peter decided he had to do something—that he had to come here in search of them both. So here he was, in this sopping tent, waiting for something to strike him.

The rain didn't let off. It kept up its consistent tapping against the canvas. At certain points throughout the afternoon Peter was certain that it had stopped and he would look out through the flap only to see it still drizzling. He thought again about returning, going back to The Ditcher's, but he knew—realistically—it was too late, too far for him to walk in the dark. Even with a torch he wouldn't trust himself not to topple over the edge of the pass.

He sat there drenched as the evening gloom stalked upon him. He kept the flap of the tent open, looking out, intent on seeing something, anything.

It got cold quickly after the sun went down. Peter remained upright, feet sticking out of the entrance of the tent, resting his heels in the saturated grass. Moonlight set the clouds in a steady luminescence. Every so often, through the gaps in cloud, he got a clear look at the moon. It reminded him of someone peeking through the curtains on a dark night. Out here he was all alone. Why had he come at all?

Around what he presumed to be midnight, he finished off the rest of his—now cold—coffee and then got into his sleeping bag, which resembled a sock fresh out of the washing machine. He tried to take his mind off the toe-curling sensation of the damp material against his skin—tried not to think that this might be how touching Rebecca's dead skin would feel.

His whole body ached and, despite everything, he managed to float away into a kind of half doze, not sleep but not quite waking either. He had no dreams, just a sequence of geometrical shapes, coloured without meaning, flashing upon his consciousness.

Feeling that the rain had stopped, he propped himself up on his elbows. He listened hard. There was no more pattering of raindrops on canvas, just the odd *drip-drip* as water trickled off the roof of the tent. He shrugged off the sleeping bag and crawled to the opening. He stuck his head out into the cool night air. He could hear something—he was certain. He strained his hearing.

Out there, somewhere, a twig snapped.

For Peter, though, in the almost silence, it might as well have been a breaking bone.

His stomach clenched and a shiver, unrelated to the chill, gripped his body. Most likely it was just an animal. Most likely. He stared into the near darkness and fumbled for the torch he kept in the front pocket of his backpack. He snapped it on and shone the beam.

As he arced the tiny yellow circle through the gloom it reflected the beads of rainwater which clung to the blades of grass. He kept up his search, running the light up the side of the sheer cliff then up to the pass. There was nothing of course. Peter was alone out here.

He turned the torchlight into his tent and laid it down on his sleeping mat. The migraine which had been threatening all day took full control of his skull. His brain throbbed away. He rubbed his eyes with his thumbs and breathed in deep, already feeling a cold taking control of his chest—a rattle getting into his throat. This had been a big mistake. He should've just forgotten all about this, left things as they were. It would be so embarrassing if he went missing too and they had to call out a mountain rescue team just because he'd got himself too ill to move.

There was a *squelch* in the distance.

He snatched up the torch and shone it off in the direction of the sound. Again, there was nothing for him to see. There would be wild deer all round these parts. He wondered whether they ordinarily came out at night. If it weren't a deer what could it possibly be?

With his heart pounding against his ribs, he lay back down on his sleeping bag, too cold and miserable to face the prospect of prising himself back into that wet fabric. He kept the torch on for a while and then, when he felt himself drifting away, he thought about saving the battery and clicked it off.

As he lay there in the darkness, only the light breeze in the trees and the thrum of the cold wreaking havoc with his system, he picked out the sounds again. More animals finding their way through the field. Perhaps they were just curious. And what was he but an animal too? What was he afraid for?

All at once the ceiling of his tent caved in and a blunted, heavy object battered down onto his forehead.

He blacked out.

4

IT SMELLED OF DAMP WOOD. Peter opened his eyes. He was in a cabin. A log cabin. He was sitting on a hard wooden chair. Its back jutted into his. His temples pulsed. A welt pounded out from his forehead where he'd been struck.

A small candle flickered away in the corner, sending uneven light dancing all round him, chasing the shadows and then ceding to them—darkness and light shifted back and forth, like the tide. The light rendered the two windows tar-black. He could see out of neither.

He tried to move his hands, but found they were bound with blue rope. He attempted to get up, but he found his feet, too, were tied to the legs of the chair. He could, however, move his neck and open his mouth. He called out. Once. Twice. One last time, before he heard the *creak* of weathered floorboards beneath the weight of footsteps.

As he twisted his body he took in the two figures who wandered in. The man and woman he had seen earlier today, on the trail, followed soon after by the black dog, its tail wagging and tongue lolling, as if this situation were nothing at all.

The woman wore a wiry woollen jumper. Her cheeks were flushed. Only then did Peter realise that it was actually warm in the cabin. She placed her hands on her hips and clucked her tongue. "So you're the *boy*friend," she said.

Peter was so shocked that he couldn't find any words.

"Yes," the woman said, scowling. "I thought you would come looking. Darren said you would."

This time Peter managed to clear his throat. "You . . . you know Darren?"

She snorted. "He was my husband. My first husband."

The man—her current husband—stood at her shoulder. He held his arm behind his back, clutching something out of sight.

Peter stared at the both of them. "Why've you tied me up?"

She shrugged. "It's easier this way—cleaner."

"'Cleaner,' how?"

The man brought his hand before him. He held an axe—what they used to cut firewood round here, Peter supposed.

"What's that for?" Peter said, already getting the feeling that he had an inkling.

The dog sniffed round Peter's feet and then licked his ankle.

The woman twitched her nose. "It took a lot of trouble to bring Rebecca out here. You see, her *father* spent a good amount of his life poisoning her against me. He told her that if I ever contacted her that she should ignore me, phone the police." She grinned. "But I convinced her in the end."

Tears welled in Peter's throat. "What have you done with her?"

"'Done with her?'" she said, arching an eyebrow.

"You've killed her!"

The woman tilted her head back. "Becky? Becky? Get out here, will you?"

More footsteps passed along the floorboards and then, to Peter's utter disbelief, Rebecca appeared in the doorway and then stood before him. She was fine. Totally fine. She looked just the same as the last day he had seen her. She smiled weakly.

Peter's mouth latched open.

Rebecca's eyes darted over him. "I'm sorry about this, Peter, but there was no other way. We couldn't get Daddy here without doing something like this."

"Something like what?"

"I had to go missing, otherwise he never would've come. We couldn't trap him."

The woman—Rebecca's mother—strode up behind her and laid her hand on her daughter's shoulder. "You can't keep a mother and daughter separate—it's against nature. Darren knew that deep down."

Peter ogled the two of them, and then examined the blade of the axe. "Why . . . why are you going to kill me?"

"Dear," Rebecca's mother said, "it's too late now, you know too much. If only you'd taken my offer this afternoon, gone back to The Ditcher's you would've been safe. But you had to come here, you had to get in the way. We can't let you live. It just won't work."

Peter yanked at his ropes—first those binding his wrists and then those binding his legs. He could only get the chair to buck up and down, but he found no purchase. He glared at them. "What did you do with Darren's body?"

Rebecca and her mother snuggled close, then her mother said, "Oh, you'll find out soon enough, dear, really don't stress too much —look at it this way, there's nothing you can do now."

The dog licked at his kneecap and Peter gazed into its matted, dead eyes, that look which showed its affection.

And its hunger.

TIME FOR FAILURE

1

THINGS HADN'T GONE too great in the past few weeks for Lauren Richardson.

She had to admit that much.

It had all started when she'd begun to get the results back from her latest exams, the ones which would either see her entering her chosen profession of medicine, or see her doing something else. She wasn't quite sure how it had happened. The fact of the matter was that she had passed just about every exam right up until this moment.

Aced them actually, though she did her best to remind herself to stay grounded.

Not to be arrogant.

She had never wanted to be *that* student.

The one who shoves their results in everybody else's faces as if a mark on a piece of paper was anything more than it sounded.

When Lauren had ventured into the Administrative Office at her university, the air had smelled of glue and paper, and the secretary's too-strong lavender perfume. Lauren had dished out her details to the secretary and the secretary had gone digging about for her results. Lots of sliding of drawers and the secretary's mumblings under her breath.

Dim daylight passed into the room through the dangling, slatted blinds at the window. The light within the room was supplemented by the flicker of the luminescent bulb which hung down from the ceiling above, giving off even, too-bright light.

Even though Lauren had ambitions to be a doctor—to spend her time within windowless rooms with those very same lights—she hadn't yet got used to them.

When Lauren had got the crisp white envelope back, her name

tidily printed out there along with her course code, she had *presumed* that it would be nothing but plain-sailing.

The same all over again.

But she had been wrong.

As she'd slit the flap of the envelope open with her index finger, she had cut herself. Blood had welled in the crease of her finger. It had blotched onto the white paper. Soaked itself into both the envelope and her results themselves.

She recalled the copper smell of blood, and the drama of the sharp pain which didn't seem to quite match the tiny little cut the paper had made in her skin.

She wasn't grossed out by blood, of course, she had got past that a *long* time ago.

In fact, that was one of the factors which had driven her on into medicine, thinking that this—rarest of gifts—might mean that something somewhere—or someone?—had preordained this career for her.

But, sucking on her cut finger, tasting the blood in her mouth, she had slipped the folded piece of now-blood-stained paper out from within, opened it up and seen the truth.

She had failed.

No, not just *failed* . . . but failed *badly*.

Out of a hundred, the passing score was sixty, and she had only managed thirty-five.

At first she had stood there, forgetting her finger for a moment until she heard a minute *drip* as her blood fell to the ground. She jabbed her finger back in between her lips and continued to suck at it as she considered the implications of that thirty-five.

Well, it was a *mistake*.

Wasn't it?

This couldn't be right.

She hadn't passed by anything *but* flying colours her entire academic career.

Even back when she'd been a kid, back in pre-school, she had always come home bearing a whole host of golden stars. In school she had picked up nothing but A's, and special commendations to boot. But now—*now*—it seemed like it had all come to an end.

She was staring failure right in the face.

Was this her *time* for failure now?

She snapped back to her senses soon afterwards, and she glanced about her as if the person responsible might be in range.

But the only person present here was the secretary.

So that was who she rounded upon.

The secretary, having already dished out the envelope containing Lauren's results, had returned to her computer monitor, and she was tapping away with great vigour at something or other. Lauren watched, hypnotised momentarily, as the secretary's long fingernails scrabbled over the plastic keys in a way which put Lauren in mind of a cat doing its best to type at a keyboard.

"Excuse me?" Lauren said, her voice coming out much weaker than she had intended.

The secretary smashed the spacebar with her thumb and then glanced up. She gave one of those vague smiles which says: *Look, I'm busy, don't shoot the messenger, okay?*

But Lauren tried to put that to one side.

"I was wondering," Lauren continued, "Who I need to talk to about my results—if there's been a, uh"—Lauren noticed how the secretary's eyes dipped down to the envelope, and to the paper which was now stained with Lauren's blood—"*mistake*," Lauren finally got out.

The secretary continued to stare at either the envelope which Lauren clutched in her hands, or the blood-stained letter, and then, slowly, she turned her attention upwards, back to Lauren. Her smile remained but Lauren could tell, from her tone of voice, that it was only for appearances. "I'll go get you a plaster, sweetie."

The secretary got up and headed off to fetch a red, plastic first aid kit which sat on the windowsill across the office.

Lauren found herself staring blankly down at the bloody letter, with *those* results all written out upon them. And she found her mind stuck with the thought—saying it over and over again: *Why me?*

Why me?

2

LAUREN MADE LITTLE PROGRESS in getting answers to just what had gone on with her results. The secretary handed her a piece of paper with the phone number and email of the Exams Officer in charge of the tests she'd just taken. When Lauren went up to go and see the man: Doctor Hendrickson, she found herself facing up to a whole lot of eyebrow arching and shaking of the head. He seemed to think that she was simply having a hard time in accepting that—for the first time—she had failed. All he seemed to encourage her to do was wait for the next batch of results to come out and see how she'd got on.

It was still possible that she would pass overall, of course.

And so Lauren did wait for the next batch of results to come out.

She went down to the Administrative Office and got the fresh, white envelope from the secretary. This time Lauren made sure not to cut herself while opening it up. When she looked inside of the envelope she found that she had got only forty-one out of a hundred.

This time, without so much as calling or emailing to make an appointment, she headed right up to Doctor Hendrickson's office.

She knocked hard on the door—harder than she had intended.

She couldn't quite keep her anger restrained within her.

Inside the office, on the other side of the door, she could hear a whole load of rustling of paper. No doubt Hendrickson was leafing through his paper records to see if he had a meeting scheduled that he had somehow overlooked. She waited another few moments before the reluctant, "Come in," command came.

When Lauren stepped into the office, she was surprised at how warm it was. It must've been something of a sun trap when the sun was out in the mornings. Dust rose up in the air and she could feel it tickling the back of her throat, suggesting that she might be on the brink of sneezing at any moment.

The office wasn't much more than a broom cupboard arrangement. Hendrickson was a new appointment. He didn't have so much as a single grey hair yet, and she guessed those sorts of things counted against an academic in his first years of appointment.

Hendrickson scowled at her from behind his untidy desk. He had several pages before him and he gripped a yellow highlighter pen as if caught in the middle of making a note. "Did you make an appointment?" he said.

Lauren sidestepped the question. Though she didn't want to come across as aggressive, she couldn't quite contain the fury which boiled her blood. She slapped the page with her latest results down on Hendrickson's desk.

Hendrickson seemed caught up with fury for a couple of moments. But then—perhaps because she was a *girl*—he allowed the impertinence to slide, and glanced down at the page. He pursed his lips, blinked a couple of times at the page, and then, with a steady hand, reached out and slid the paper back at Lauren. "I'm sorry," he said, "if you wish to discuss your results then I'm afraid you'll need to make an appointment—just like everybody else."

Hendrickson returned his attention to the pages he had spread before him, shaking his head and uttering something under his breath that Lauren couldn't catch.

But Lauren wasn't moving anywhere.

"This," she said, "is nothing short of sabotage. There's somebody out there trying to get to me—I know it."

Hendrickson flashed his eyebrows, but kept on staring down at his papers.

He wanted her to leave.

He didn't want these complications.

But Lauren knew that if she was to get answers then she needed to be insistent. "Look," Lauren said, "I studied hard for those exams, just like *every* exam I've ever taken. I can *tell* if I've done well on a test, or not. I know if I've grasped the material." She nodded at the page which contained her results. "And I can tell you that this mark *isn't right*."

Hendrickson continued to peruse the pages before him, swiped at a line of text with his highlighter pen, leaving a fluorescent sash of yellow, and then he glanced up at her, his head slightly cocked to one side. "Listen here, young lady"—Lauren really didn't know how he got off calling her 'young lady' since she was perhaps only ten years younger than he was—"let me tell you a little story about *high achievers.*"

Lauren couldn't quite get her head around the contempt in his voice when he spoke the words 'high achievers,' all that seemed to be missing was for Hendrickson to make quotation marks with his fingers.

Hendrickson continued, unabated, "There comes a time, in everybody's academic career, when they reach a *plateau*—when they reach a stage in their education where they simply cannot get their head around some basic point or principle." Hendrickson gave a self-satisfied grin, and then added, "It happens to the best of us, and the only way forwards is to track back—to return to our educational texts, or ask for assistance from our tutors. *That,*" he added, with a note of finality, "is the way forward."

Lauren knew, beyond the condescending tone, that Hendrickson was telling the truth. She had experienced plateaus before, she knew that, but, at the same time, she knew that she was good at recognising where she hadn't quite grasped some specific part of a subject.

She *would* do just as he suggested.

She would 'track back' through the material.

Make sure she was acquainted with it as thoroughly as possible.

And then she would perform well on the exam.

For these specific exams—the exams in question—she knew,

AV IAIN

without a doubt in her own mind, that she had gone through the same process as before.

She had *known* the subject matter.

Inside and out.

That was the issue here.

But, somehow, she needed to make Hendrickson understand.

Still, she was having a hard time keeping her anger in check . . . but, then again, why *should* she keep her anger in check when it was *her* future at stake?

"Who marked these exams?" Lauren said.

Hendrickson had now turned a shade of puce. He seemed to have given up on pretending to skim through the pages before him. His gaze was filled with fury. "I'm not at liberty to say," he said, sharply. "And, Miss Richardson, if you *do not* leave this office right at this very moment, then you shall find yourself in a great deal of trouble."

Lauren batted off this threat. "Who else can I speak to?"

Hendrickson rolled his eyes and shook his head. He gave a nonchalant smile. "Really, Miss Richardson, you'd be much better advised to simply let the matter drop and return to your learning." He paused a moment, and his tone hardened all of a sudden. "Before you burn any bridges."

"Who. Can. I. Speak. To?"

Hendrickson held her gaze for several moments, and then, with a profound sigh, he dug about in his desk drawer. He produced a scrap of paper and a pen. With a few clicks of his mouse—a few scurries over his keyboard—he produced something on screen, unseen to Lauren, and then copied it down onto the piece of paper.

Finished scribbling out the name and number, he thrust the paper at Lauren. "Here," he said, and then, in a lower voice, "Now get out of my hair."

Lauren put on her best false smile—the one that she would put on when she'd been a little girl and been forced to stand next to

82

some body-odour-, and halitosis-stinking uncle for a photo. "Thank you for your time, *doctor*."

On her way out of the office, she slammed the door so hard that she set off a car alarm in the car park which sat alongside the building.

3

LAUREN'S ENQUIRIES took her a whole bunch of places about campus. It seemed that the person who Hendrickson had given her the contact details of was somewhat elusive. At first, Lauren presumed the worst and thought that Hendrickson had simply given her a wild-goose chase. That he had simply made somebody up for Lauren to follow about. Reasoning this out further, though, Lauren decided to herself that this wouldn't have been a particularly smart move if 'getting her out of his hair' was his main goal.

In the end, Lauren managed to track Mrs Helen Dunwitch—the name written on the scrap of paper—to a far corner of the campus. She was in charge of what was described, on the steel label on her door, as Assessment Coordination. Just as before, Lauren knocked on the door and awaited a response. It was only when a post-graduate student came down a staircase and informed her that Mrs Helen Dunwitch had already gone home for the weekend that Lauren realised that she had reached a dead-end.

For now.

Lauren buzzed back out of *that* building and then slumped down onto the concrete steps. She sat there for a long while, her knees crumpled up to her chest. She stared out across the greenery of the campus. She hadn't even realised that it was a Friday. She had been so preoccupied with this whole results thing that she hadn't so much as noted the day of the week. And she had been so caught up chasing her results that she realised she'd missed her afternoon lecture. She checked her watch just to make sure. It was already past five in the evening. Her lecture had finished about ten minutes ago.

What was she going to do?

Her brain felt stressed with the whole business of the day. She was so certain that the results were wrong . . . that somebody—*some-*

where—had taken against her for whatever reason. And she knew that she wouldn't be able to sleep till she knew the truth.

That was the fact of the matter.

And it was then that the idea dawned on Lauren.

It seemed so obvious now.

Like there was no other option.

She lugged herself back to her feet, headed back into the building which housed Mrs Helen Dunwitch's office. When she approached the door, she looked about quickly, seeing if there was anybody still about. But, it seemed, as she noted with just about any office—*anywhere*—that since the boss had gone home, the rest of the employees had followed suit.

This was her chance.

Time for her to find out what had really happened.

And with nobody to stop her.

She reached out and turned the doorknob to the office.

It wasn't locked.

Quickly, she slid in side-on through the doorway, and soon found herself standing in Mrs Helen Dunwitch's office.

The office was much bigger than Hendrickson's, and though there was a large window, it was covered up by blinds. Lauren guessed that Mrs Helen Dunwitch didn't appreciate anybody looking into her office while she wasn't in there.

Lauren flipped on the desk lamp, which immediately illuminated the room in a strong, yellow light. There were bookshelves all around—occupying every wall—and they were stuffed full with various papers and hard-backed manuals. They had all those human resources titles—the ones which made her shudder—and she looked away from them before she had fully a chance to absorb them.

The computer was switched off and when Lauren turned it back on she was greeted with a password screen. She looked about quickly for a Post-It that Mrs Helen Dunwitch might've pasted up on the monitor or on the desktop, but it seemed that Mrs Helen Dunwitch took her security a little more seriously than most. There was no sign of any login credentials.

Lauren looked about her, identified a filing cabinet.

Though Mrs Helen Dunwitch was meticulous with her digital security, she had left the key to the filing cabinet dangling from its bobbly, metal chain, and so all Lauren needed to do was slip it into the slot and turn it.

The mechanism clicked open.

As Lauren flipped through the first drawer of files, she wondered—just for a second—how much trouble she might get into if somebody happened to walk in on her now.

Would they throw her out of the university?

There would be disciplinary action, no doubt.

If she was proved to have tampered with exam results—or even to have been looking through them.

But it was too late now.

She had already opened the drawer.

Now the files were right here.

She could get her answers.

It was much easier than she would've thought to find the file separator for the exams she had just taken. They used the same code which she had memorised to write on the top of her exam papers. When she'd located that, it was a simple matter of locating the manuscripts held within. The names were alphabetised and Lauren found 'Richardson' without much trouble.

She pulled her file and found herself staring at her exam paper.

She checked through the lines of her answer, and—sure enough—it was alive with a sea of red crosses: here, there, and all over the place.

She leafed through the pages, got to the end and found a pair of initials scrawled there.

AJ

She said those initials over in her mind a couple of times. They wouldn't be too easy to forget. Then she slid her exam paper back into its place.

Outside the office, she heard some stirring.

A *clack-clack* of wood on wood.

Lauren startled. Glanced back over her shoulder. Concentrated on the source of the sound. Listened out for another sound.

And then—*horror of horrors!*—she watched the door to the office creaking open.

It was then that Lauren found herself staring right back at a cleaner.

The woman seemed to be in her fifties, and she gripped tight to a broom with pudgy fists. She squinted at Lauren, right away surely knowing that Lauren shouldn't be there.

Lauren's heart bounced up into her throat. Her blood ran cold. A sweat broke out over the whole surface of her skin.

The cleaner's stern expression cracked into a smile. "Sorry, dearie," she said, "didn't think there was nobody in here," and then she left Lauren alone again.

Lauren stood stock still in Mrs Helen Dunwitch's office, listening to the cleaner moving off into another area of the building, and then, breaking out of her static position, she bolted from the office.

In her mind, she repeated, over and over: *AJ, AJ, AJ.*

4

LAUREN REALLY had reached the end of things by the time she'd got the initials AJ, and she realised that there was little choice for her now but to go home. So she did. And it was while she was sitting on the bus that she caught sight of one of the boys on her course: Terry.

Terry had jet-black hair which hung down to the pit of his chin. His eyes were slightly lazy—the way that they lolled about their sockets, and how his eyelids seemed to be constantly drooping. But Lauren knew that Terry was also one of the brightest—if not *the* brightest—student on her course.

As the gentle *hum* of the bus engine rumbled on around her, she took up a place on the seat beside Terry. Just like always, a thick scent of musk piped through the ventilation ducts of the bus. She felt a little nauseous, and the twists and turns weren't doing her any good.

Perhaps she was still flustered from all that had gone on that day, or maybe she thought that Terry was trustworthy. Whatever it was, she found herself opening up to Terry about her results, about what had happened.

She said nothing about having stolen into Mrs Helen Dunwitch's office, however.

That was the one part that she left out.

With her cathartic outpouring done with, Lauren looked to Terry for his response.

For several moments, he remained still, as if her story hadn't caused so much as a surface-level reaction in him. But Lauren knew this reaction in Terry. She saw it whenever a teacher would pick him out for a particularly tricky question—no doubt wanting to bring Terry down a peg or two. When asked the question, Terry would clam up. It would seem that he was completely stumped over the answer, and then he would reel out some perfect explanation, or observation. Something that would blow everybody away.

The teacher included.

Terry pursed his lips, glanced back at Lauren briefly. "You said that it's something personal—that you believe somebody has a vendetta against you?"

Lauren wasn't sure that she would've chosen exactly the word 'vendetta,' but she nodded along all the same.

Terry broke off their stare and gazed out the window, into the darkened side alleys as they passed by. "Then—the way I see it— you've got to work out just who might've been involved with all this. Who might've had the initials 'AJ.'"

Though Lauren had told Terry about the initials, she had claimed that she had got them off Doctor Hendrickson. She had hoped, somewhat vaguely, that Terry might be able to recall some-body with those initials.

Terry remained still, continuing to stare out through the glass into the night-time. Lauren wondered if he was going to add some-thing else, if there was some masterstroke that he was just biding his time with, ready to strike out with at any moment.

But, no, he remained silent for the rest of the journey, and, when they reached his stop, Terry got up from his seat, reached out and shook her hand in that antiquated style of his, and said, "Best of luck fixing this." He was about to head off along the aisle of the bus, and out through the folded-back doors before he paused, and added, "Remember, it might be the most innocuous thing. Just some tiny little moment that you thought nothing of. But it might well have meant an awful lot to somebody else—to this *AJ*."

And, with that, he gave Lauren a stern nod, grasped his beaten-and-battered leather satchel beneath his arm and then headed on off out the bus and into the night.

Lauren clasped her eyes shut and pressed her fingers into the recesses of her forehead.

Forcing herself to think.

5

NOTHING CAME TO LAUREN until late on Sunday night. Though she had wreaked considerable brain power on the matter all day Saturday—and most of Sunday—she hadn't been able to come up with a likely suspect.

Simply nobody leaped to mind.

And so she turned her attention back to work, back to her text-book. She just wanted to forget about the whole unpleasant incident now, and she couldn't help wondering if she'd—*just maybe*—been arrogant with that whole thing involving Doctor Hendrickson.

Maybe he was right.

Maybe she *had* 'plateaued.'

And yet she'd been so certain that she'd aced the test.

All the tests.

Could it be that she was really delusional?

As all these thoughts tumbled through her mind, Lauren brain-lessly copied out page after page of her medical textbook, losing herself in the mechanics of transferring the words from the glossy textbook pages onto the lined paper before her. Almost subcon-sciously, the information written out there tumbled through her brain. She often wondered if any of this information stuck, but she had realised—after doing this for nigh-on twenty years of her acad-emic career now—that it would all come back to her in the exam.

Or at times when she least expected it.

She had simply learned to give herself up to the process.

And Lauren had just got through her twelfth page for the evening when she felt something snap in her mind. Some little frag-ment. But *something*. Though she felt like screeching out, *"Eureka!"* at the tops of her lungs, something deep within reminded her that she had neighbours surrounding who might already be asleep.

So she simply turned the page of her notepad, and began to scribble away.

Not wanting to forget any of the details.

6

LAUREN WROTE LONG into the night—wrote away for maybe two hours. It was important for her to get everything out of the way here. She had everything in mind now. *All* of it. Right down to the all-important details. The little things which would give her credibility.

Only when she sat back from the page, glanced at the clock, did she realise that she had been writing out by hand a blow-by-blow account of the incident for two straight hours.

And seeing the whole incident scrawled out there in her handwriting seemed to make it real. Seemed to make the idea that she *could* fight back at against this injustice—and this *was* injustice—a little more real.

The incident, as it had come to her, had been so lucid.

And yet, at one stage, it had all seemed so lost.

But she had it down there on paper now.

All scribbled out so that she would never forget it.

Simply the act of writing it out—Lauren knew—would make it stick in her brain for the rest of her life.

Her brain felt like it was hopping with electricity—like the neurons were bouncing back and forth like a series of runaway trains. She stared at the page of her writing and felt the images forming within her mind. The blue ink taking form into something approaching a film reel. And all she had to do was sit back here, at her desk, and watch.

7

I T HAD BEEN EARLY.

Six—or seven?—in the morning.

One of those biting-cold days.

Frost on the pavements.

Frost webbing the leaves on the trees.

That slightly bloody scent in her nostrils.

The one which warned her that she had a cold coming on.

Her trainers crunched against the frosty ground—*crunched* over the iced-over puddles of water.

Lauren could still taste the remnants of her peanut-butter-on-toast breakfast

The sour taste of coffee at the back of her throat.

Everything around her seemed a kind of bluish glow.

Up ahead, Lauren could see the entrance to the Repository.

That was the name they gave it.

Among the medical students.

Lauren flashed her plastic access card against the reader. The machine beeped her in with a flat note, and blinked a green light at her.

Lauren passed in through the sliding-back doors.

She went through the normal routine.

Put on a white coat.

The shoe protectors.

Hairnet.

Lauren had arrived here first.

She always got here first.

A matter of pride for her.

She stepped through another set of doors.

Emerged into a large room.

Already it was lit with the fluorescent glow of a strip bulb up over her head.

The four white tables all scrubbed down.

Ready to go.

Soon they would be standing here.

Around the tables.

Dissecting cadavers.

Lauren had thought she was alone and then—all of a sudden— she realised that she was not. The voice was cheery. Bright and perky. *Too* bright and perky given the death which hung about this place.

Lauren turned to look.

A member of staff.

One of the members of staff who'd often hung about here.

She had never really known what he did.

He wasn't much older than her. He had blond hair buzzed short. His eyes were blue. And his white coat hung limply off his lacerated frame.

Something about him . . . something about him that . . .

Before Lauren could complete the thought, the member of staff caught her in his gaze. He gave her a sly smile. "Morning," he said, that bright tone grating on Lauren so much.

"Uh, hi," Lauren said, very aware that they were all alone.

Though she had made it a point of personal pride to arrive here —to the Repository—earlier than the rest of her class, it was never because she wanted a monopoly on the tutors' time. More likely that she just wanted to be alone for a moment.

A quiet pause for reflection.

But this member of staff here, he had shattered that for her now.

The member of staff took a couple of steps towards her.

A couple of steps *too* close.

Lauren could smell sardines on his breath. She wondered at how she had managed to make her observation so precise. How it was *sardines* and not some other stinking fish.

But she just knew.

Another step.

Two.

Three.

Four . . .

He stood only a couple of paces away from her now. The stench of his breath was almost too much to bear, and Lauren was struggling to be polite. She was struggling not to simply buckle over and gasp for air. Perhaps it was in that moment that she happened to glance down to the breast pocket of the member of staff's white coat. To see the badge which was pinned there. The badge which read: Adam Jackson.

AJ.

Him.

Lauren broke off her gaze at the badge. Jerked her chin upwards. Forced herself to meet his eye. The member of staff— Adam Jackson, *AJ*—was smirking strongly now. He reached out and touched her on the upper part of her arm.

"Got the shakes?" he said.

Lauren felt herself flinch beneath his touch.

"It's all right," Adam Jackson continued, "We all get them from time to time. At the beginning."

Lauren wanted to tell him that she was fine. That she had no trouble. That she didn't *need* him to be *touching* her right now. And yet she just couldn't vocalise any of it.

"You're a nice girl," he said. "Very nice girl—would a nice girl like you have a boyfriend?"

Lauren blinked a couple of times, out of disbelief. "No," she said, the word almost dying in her throat.

Adam Jackson seemed to sense her discomfort. He removed his

fingertips from her arm. "There, there," he said, "Just making conversation, just trying to make you feel a little better, that's *all*."

"I'm . . . I'm fine," Lauren finally got out.

She glanced about the room, hoping that there might be a security camera, or *something*.

She did spot one, over in the corner of the room.

She wondered if it was getting all this.

Or if they were too far away to be seen.

Did it really matter?

It wasn't like this Adam Jackson had *done* anything.

Lauren wasn't sure when she'd done it, but—somehow—she had managed to turned her back to Adam Jackson. She had turned her attention onto a poster which hung up on the wall opposite. And she was staring at it as if it might have the power to steal her away from this place. To pop her somewhere *safe*.

And it was then that she felt his touch again.

This time on the outside of her leg.

Working its way inwards.

To her backside.

Alarm bells rang out through her mind, and yet she couldn't act on it.

Was this what they called a rabbit in headlights?

She had always thought of herself as being better than that.

As being stronger than that.

Was she really nothing more than a spooked animal?

He continued to touch her, and Lauren knew that she had to turn around.

That she had to do *something*.

But she just stayed still.

Wouldn't move a muscle.

And then, inside of her, something *did* snap.

Lauren felt the heat right down at the base of her belly. She felt it become so hot that she thought it might scorch its way through her skin. She caught sight of the flask—a *glass* flask—and she snatched for it. With a single *tinkle* of breaking glass, she grabbed one of the shards, spun around and held it up to Adam Jackson's throat.

Adam Jackson's creeping hands left her. His expression turned from one of lechery to one of shock. He backed up from her. His eyes never leaving hers. He held up his hands as if they'd been suddenly transported to a Western. His shock descended into him and a surly smile replaced it. "Okay," he said, "Just take it easy—all right? Nobody needs to know about this. Nobody needs to find out."

Lauren grasped the broken glass tighter still. She could feel it biting into her hand. She could smell the blood cutting through the air. But, at the same time, she couldn't turn her attention away from Adam Jackson . . . he might do it again.

He *would* do it again.

Of that she was sure.

"Come on," Adam Jackson said to her, his focus suddenly snapping onto her bleeding hand—where the glass was sinking into her skin, "Let's go and get that seen to, huh?"

Lauren was ready for him to touch her again, and she was sure she would kill him.

Certain that she would.

But he didn't make to touch her.

He simply padded away.

Already, Lauren could feel her mind squeezing tight, and then relaxing, just like a bicep being pumped with weights. And she found herself following on his heels. Like nothing more than a mist floating on a chilly breeze. She couldn't stop herself.

When he had bandaged her hand, Lauren sat on the edge of the rickety doctor's bench, a green, paper sheet beneath her. She stared at her bandaged hand. At how a little of the blood seeped through the white cotton.

Off down the corridor, she could hear voices.

Could hear *his* voice.

Adam Jackson.

His voice wound through the air, twisting through the sharp scent of alcohol.

The bitter odour of disinfectant.

He was *speaking* to somebody.

". . . Nothing . . . really, it was nothing at all . . . yes, you can speak with him if you like . . . I think you'll find . . ."

But then the words were gone.

And it was as if Lauren was forgetting the incident afresh.

As if she was assigning the whole sorry affair to some distant basement of her mind.

Never to be opened without the right tools.

L AUREN SAT BACK from the desk. She stared down at the pages.

It was odd.

The feeling of *guilt*.

She tried to pin it down, to work out just what it might mean.

Did she feel guilty for not having said a word—not to anyone— or did she feel guilty because she had forgotten? That she had filed away the incident. Told herself to forget about it . . . and wouldn't it have stayed forgotten, if it wasn't for those initials?

If it wasn't for *AJ*.

Adam Jackson.

Lauren pulled herself into bed sometime after midnight.

Another Monday had crept up on her.

Just like that.

There never seemed enough time to get everything done.

And almost by the time that thought had skittered through her mind, Lauren could already see another day dawning. The pinkish glow of light making its way about the fringes of her curtains. Though she had hardly slept at all, she felt, if not *refreshed*, then *invigorated*.

She knew that she would get to the bottom of this.

And now.

After a long spell in the shower, making sure that she got herself as clean as she could, Lauren headed to the Repository. She made straight for the room she had passed by every time she'd wandered into the place. Where a security guard sat with a bank of screens before him. The security guard glanced up at Lauren, seemingly more surprised that she had so much as noticed him. Lauren thought to herself about how she had never said so much as a simple good morning to the man. He smiled at her now, though, not a kind smile, but a *polite* smile all the same. He touched the brim of his baseball cap and said, "Miss? How can I help you then?"

"A tape," Lauren said, "I'm looking for a tape."

The security guard furrowed his brow. "Security tape?"

"Yes," she said.

The security guard sat forwards in his chair. He tugged at the brim of his cap, and then said, "Might I ask on whose behalf you're asking?"

Without thinking, Lauren said, "Mrs Helen Dunwitch."

"Mrs Dunwitch?" the security guard repeated, his eyes glazing over.

For a second, Lauren was sure that the security guard was going to challenge her further.

That he might place a call to Mrs Helen Dunwitch to check up that this was a legitimate request.

But the security guard was already reaching over for a scuffed leather-bound book and flipping through the pages. "Date?" he said, without looking up.

Lauren told him when it had happened.

The security guard stopped turning the pages. He glanced up at her. Then he shook his head. "Sorry," he said, "Only keep tapes back-dated for a month, then they get rewritten."

Lauren felt her heart sink. Her blood cooled all through her body, and a horrible dizzy feeling descended on her. But she remained calm, detached, as she said, "Could you check the entry?"

The security guard tilted his head to one side in a way which said—to Lauren—that he would humour her all the same, but that the systems here were fool proof.

When the security guard turned to the page of the entry Lauren requested, however, he furrowed his eyebrows. He squinted down at the entry. "Huh," he said, more out of genuine surprise than incomprehension. "Looks like that tape of yours was checked out."

"'Checked out?'" Lauren said. "By who?"

The security guard stared long and hard at the page for several moments, and then, just as Lauren was certain that he was going to ask some searching questions about her credentials, he read off the name written there beside the signature, "Doctor Hendrickson."

9

LAUREN'S FEET hardly touched the floor on the way to Doctor Hendrickson's office. She could feel her pulse beating hard in her mouth. She had her fists bunched down at her sides and she wasn't sure what she was going to do. With every step of the way, she was certain that somebody was going to show up to stop her. That she wouldn't be allowed up the stairs to Doctor Hendrickson's office. But nobody did stop her. Only Doctor Hendrickson's locked office door stopped her.

Lauren twisted the door knob several times. It was locked. She tried again. And again. Getting angrier and angrier as she did so. And then she stood still. She pressed her ear up against the door. Listened for any sound on the other side.

Nothing.

She listened a little harder.

Could she hear breathing?

She was almost certain that she could hear breathing.

Or was it just her imagination?

She eyed up the door, thought about how she might be able to bust it down.

Behind her, she caught sight of a fire extinguisher. She knew, if she really had to, she could use it to get inside. Would that compromise her? Would the tape be valid evidence if she had used criminal means to get hold of it?

She had no idea . . . and she was an aspiring *doctor*, not a lawyer, after all.

As Lauren considered her options, she watched on with slight disbelief as the door knob of Doctor Hendrickson's office turned, and the door slowly creaked open.

She stood and stared.

Caught Doctor Hendrickson's eyes between the crack.

He stared back at her.

Made to close the door.

But Lauren was too fast for him.

She stuck her foot in the crack before he could even get it so much as closed a hair's breadth. Though the door rammed against the side of her foot, Lauren knew what she had to do. That she had to stand her ground now. If she wanted answers, she had to stand her ground.

"I'm calling security!" Doctor Hendrickson said.

"I know about the tape!" Lauren blurted out.

Doctor Hendrickson continued to resist for a few seconds, and then, what she had said apparently hitting home, he relented and drew the door back into his office.

For several moments, Lauren and Doctor Hendrickson stood there regarding one another. Lauren could hardly blink for the rage which was twisting through her body. She couldn't believe just what had gone on. And she wanted answers.

She wanted them *now*.

Doctor Hendrickson stood back to allow her into his office.

Lauren swept in past him.

Doctor Hendrickson shut the door behind him and twisted the lock shut. His eyes were wide, and Lauren could see that he was somewhat flustered. But he said nothing as he rounded his desk and took up his chair. He sat there—straight-backed—and clutched his fists before him. He stared at his clutched fists as if there was something utterly fascinating about them.

"I remember," Lauren said, "What happened, that day."

Doctor Hendrickson remained fixated on his clutched fists. His attention seemed unshakeable.

"I know that it was . . . Adam Jackson . . . who marked my paper."

Doctor Hendrickson still said not a word.

Lauren wondered if she was going to have to spell out everything—if she was going to have to fill in all the gaps. But she held back. She knew that she had to give Doctor Hendrickson time. She couldn't rush anything here . . . this was what her mother might've called a 'very delicate matter.'

Doctor Hendrickson kept his voice low when he spoke—so low that Lauren wanted to ask him to speak up, but she simply couldn't summon the words . . . or perhaps she was afraid that she would resort to insults, and that would get them nowhere.

"That day," Doctor Hendrickson said, and then, his voice getting softer still, "it had nothing to do with your exams."

Lauren stared holes in Doctor Hendrickson. She could feel the blood bumbling about her veins. It felt like her head might pop at any moment.

Doctor Hendrickson glanced up at her briefly. "I looked over the paper—there was nothing amiss—you simply didn't grasp the concepts."

Lauren felt a voice deep within her screaming out, *No, no, no, no, NO!*

She was trembling all over now, and she had to work hard not to let on to Doctor Hendrickson that she was doing so . . . that she was frail, perhaps on the brink of toppling onto the floor. That would be just what he would want.

Doctor Hendrickson continued, "In fact, Adam Jackson came to me, and he asked whether it might be possible to raise your mark, so that it might not seem so . . ." he searched for words for a few seconds ". . . *conspicuous.*"

Lauren could still feel herself shaking. She knew that he was lying—that Doctor Hendrickson was *lying*, though she couldn't determine the reason.

"I *understand* the charges," Doctor Hendrickson said, "the *serious-ness* of them." He paused for a moment, and he took a dry breath. "And I realise how implicated *I* have become in all of this."

When Lauren met Doctor Hendrickson's gaze now, she saw that

he had tears in his eyes. And yet she couldn't quite keep the hum of anger from taking her over.

"I took the tape," Doctor Hendrickson said, inclining his head slightly, "in case you might wish to make a complaint at any point— I thought that it would be safer for me to keep the evidence here, in my office, for when you might ask for it." He met her eye again. "The way I understand the process, security wipes the tapes after a month or so."

It was almost like somebody had clipped a wire within her— Lauren felt the heat gradually drain from her. It gave way to an almost *normal* temperature. Her heart thumped a couple of times. She stopped shaking.

And yet she still couldn't square what Doctor Hendrickson was saying.

What he was *telling* her.

Doctor Hendrickson continued, "I only hope that you might forgive me, but I didn't think it my place to make the complaint. I may not have read the situation correctly, and Adam Jackson is my friend." He paused again, no doubt wondering just how moral the ground he was striking was. "I thought that I would leave it up to you."

With that final remark, Doctor Hendrickson got up from his seat and paced over to his bookshelf. He slipped a pair of heavy textbooks out of the way and uncovered a black plastic cassette box. He brought it over to his desk and he set it down before Lauren.

"There," he said, his tone becoming a little hardier now, "I think that's all you'll be needing."

Lauren stared at the little black cassette box for several seconds. Her heart was thumping in her eardrums now. More than anything she wanted to snatch up the cassette, take it with her, and venture on out of Doctor Hendrickson's office.

Get on with it.

But she still had a lingering question.

She turned her attention back to Doctor Hendrickson, and said, "You're telling the truth, then, about my exam?"

Doctor Hendrickson intertwined his fingers. He clutched his hands together for a few seconds, and then nodded.

Lauren nodded back at him. She felt empty inside, as if something had sucked all her blood away. She glanced down at the cassette box, picked it up, and then she headed out of the office.

10

LAUREN SAT on the concrete steps to the building which housed Doctor Hendrickson's office. She gazed out at the trees as they swayed a little in the breeze. She held the cassette in her left hand. It felt heavy—much heavier than she had expected.

Memory was a strange thing.

She had relied on it for so much—for so many of her exams.

It had got her through each and every time.

Now, though, it seemed as if it had deserted her. As if that most trusty of abilities had slipped from her grasp. How hadn't she recalled that day—with Adam Jackson—at the Repository? How had she managed to forget such an incident? Was it some sort of trauma? Perhaps, but she had the memory back now . . . and the proof to go with it. She could go to the police, have Adam Jackson answer for his actions.

Although Lauren hated to admit it, she couldn't help wishing that there had been some secret to this whole thing—to her failing marks. She had been *one-hundred-per-cent* certain that it had been a conspiracy, that somebody had had it in for her.

Or, perhaps, she had only had it in for herself.

Because she knew what Doctor Hendrickson had said was correct.

That she had plateaued.

And now it was up to her to fix it.

She was on her own.

Gripping the plastic cassette tight in her fist, she headed towards the bus stop.

She wouldn't go to any lectures today.

She needed to rethink everything.

Rethink her life.

Rethink herself.

And only then might she get back onto the right track.

DOG WALKER

I'VE BEEN DOING this for years now. It's a good business really. I get up at four thirty every morning for my eggs and bacon and then I head out to walk the dogs. It's not a bad life, but I've seen better—namely in the houses of my customers.

This one area, called The Hedges, is a real plush spot. You'll find all sorts there: bankers, brokers, accountants . . . the lot.

On my time off, generally from about four o'clock in the afternoon, I've been thinking about The Hedges a bit. In fact, I've been thinking about it constantly. I've come to the conclusion that the only intelligent thing to do is to rip it off.

My customers have no reason not to trust me.

I never finished school. I was a government-branded burden for several years. I suppose that gives them the edge on me. They believe their university degrees or their middle-class upbringings have entitled them to their life. Conditioning can be a funny thing.

Another reason is what I do. They think I'm sweet. On my tax forms it says: dog walker, and that's exactly what I do. No pretentions.

A few years back we used to have a gathering of our like, the dog walkers, on Thursday nights. I remember Paul used to call himself a 'dog trainer and stylist,' another one—I forget his name—went for 'canine specialist,' under the umbrella term of 'canine services'— sounding far too vague for my liking. But the one that topped them all was Nigel. He was a 'dog perambulator,' if you'll believe that . . .

Walking dogs puts me in my place.

The last and, perhaps, most important is my appearance. When I was younger there was no question that I frightened the living crap out of every old-aged pensioner I passed on the street at night. In my more immature years I'd jump at them as I went past, watching them flinch or, sometimes, run back up the street in fear. I even spent six months in prison for nicking. Although, that experience neither humbled me into an entirely straight existence nor formed my mind into a purely criminal trajectory. Sometimes the media just tell lies.

Anyhow, now I'm well over fifty, I have this whole trusting thing about my face. My previous hard cheeks have slunk away into old-age flab and my fierce blue eyes have been deaden by that garden growing where my eyebrows used to be. In addition to this I play to my appearance by wearing a faded blue polo shirt reading: 'Sam Longman: Dog Walker,' along with a cartooned picture of me scrubbing a dog, under mountains of foam, in an old-school iron washtub. You couldn't buy this disguise.

In a nut-shell, my clients trust me with their keys, their pure-breed dogs and—by extension—their material lives.

The *how* is an interesting one. I've already mentioned that I've got the keys. That's the first step. Bloody hell, I'd say it's a giant leap. The rest is logistics and luck.

As far as logistics is concerned, most of these apartments—or the ones I'm planning on ripping off—have underground car parks. I have a dirty great white van, with the same logo and name as on the polo shirt. That'll be no trouble, then. One thing that does worry me, however, is cameras.

Although, I'm widely trusted I know what rich people are like. It's something completely different from trust. It's really about control.

I've seen ads for cameras in the disguise of televisions, computer hard-drives, even teddy bears . . . These people might say it's about catching the maid stealing the silver, or the baby sitter slapping the kids—that's to say: getting ripped off—however, that's not what it's about at all. Not really. It's really about control. What they're getting from these devices is the satisfaction of saying, 'I control you, you're my bitch, I pay your wage and if you cheat me you're out with the rubbish tomorrow.' That's not to say that if they find someone ripping them off they're not going to fire them, of course they will, they might even go to prison. None of that scares me, but what does is being under someone else's control. I don't like that one bit, that's why I started my own business instead of working as an employee of the door-to-door dog walking service like <u>dogwalkers4you.com</u>. Don't get me started on them, though, or we'll be here all week.

So, the only question that remains now is when? Today, tomorrow, next week, just before I retire? I guess when I go through with this I'll have to retire. It would be too suspicious turning up for work on Monday, having ripped off the house the previous Friday while the owner was at work. No, I've got my eyes set on retirement: Spain.

The traditional destination for the old crook has, and always will be, somewhere in South America. It feels like you're a long way away when you're there, on the other side of the world. However, in my opinion, Spain is far enough. Also, you have the advantage that there are already so many other foreign crooks hiding out there that you'll just be one drop of sweat in a million. That's what I want: anonymity.

All this writing has got me riled up, thinking a lot. It'll be so easy.

Frightening, isn't it?

SURPRISE, SURPRISE

1

WHEN PEOPLE IN TOWN spoke about what had gone on at the previous year's summer fair, I pretty much just shut up. There was no point in me going and getting myself into trouble, after all. And yet it's the stuff of nightmares, those little things which seem to plague you forever and ever if you don't manage to get on top of them. Find a way to beat them. And yet, with some things, you just have to give it up. There *is* no way to beat them.

I remembered it all clearly, like it hadn't happened a year back —a year today, the day of the summer fair.

A year earlier, I'd been walking along with my husband, Carl, wearing the red dress that rode way too high up the knee and which stopped far too short of my breasts. I could feel the chill of the early autumn breeze breathing all over skin, bringing me out in pimples.

Though I'd already made the case to Carl that, if we weren't going home, then at least for him to allow me to head back to the car and grab a sweater, but he just kept on grinning at me, what with that eye-sparklingly way that he did, and said nothing.

So, pretty much all I could do was fold my hands over my chest.

Somehow, I got the impression that he was enjoying my discomfort.

The grass beneath our feet had long ago turned to a sort of brown mush, and I could smell mud mixed with fried electronics on the air. That was all mixed up with the candy floss and the buttered popcorn too, of course, and I couldn't quite make up my mind whether my mouth tasted deathly bitter or overly sweet.

In the end, I just opted to think that, later on, I'd dig myself out a bowl of cereal, splash it with milk, and make myself better eating my way through it.

"Hey," Carl had said, pointing.

I followed his finger, all the way to this kind of haunted house thing that he was indicating, though I had to look over the façade a couple of times to confirm it.

Like a haunted house, it had those carts on rails, what with people shuffling into it, the door bolting shut behind them. They'd then disappear behind these transparent flaps of plastic—slipping away into darkness. I watched on as they'd come out the other side a few minutes later.

The main difference, though, at least to me, was the way that, when they came out the other side, having been through the ride— which in bright yellow, blinking lights was named *Surprise, Surprise!*— the people didn't look totally bored out of their minds.

That had been what I'd expected of them.

But neither did they look terrified.

Looking over their faces again, trying to get things straight about their reaction, I realised that they looked disturbed. All shaken up. And I only had to flip a glance to Carl, standing beside me, to know that he was grinning from ear to ear.

Perhaps on a subconscious level he had observed just what I had.

He nodded to the *Surprise Surprise!* ride. "Come on," he said. "That looks fun."

Feeling another one of those crispy autumn breezes, I tightened my arms over my chest. I bit down hard into my lower lip, trying to make it hurt enough so that it'd stop me trembling all over. But I tasted blood before I stopped trembling.

As if to reassure me, Carl reached his hand around me, and clutched me tight to his chest. And then, just like that, I felt myself being *dragged* along in the direction of the ride.

2

WHEN WE GOT CLOSER UP, I noticed the owner of the ride. He was a man wearing a beaten-up tuxedo, and he had a waxed moustache with the ends drawn out into sharp points. His complexion was mottled, his cheeks webbed with broken, blood-red veins.

As he stepped over to the cart of people, those who had just ridden the ride: a teenage couple, I overheard the girl saying to the boy, "But they looked so real—I don't understand it."

The boy reassured her in that way all *boys* seemed to be compelled to do. "Oh, don't tell me that it shook you up—it was just fairground ride."

But, as I watched them walking away, the boy resting his arm about the girl's shoulders, I could see that the two of them were *both* a little shaken up by just what they'd seen on the *Surprise, Surprise!* ride.

It was then that Carl leaned into me. "You think I should've told them to use a condom?"

"Huh?" I said, away on my own little train of thought.

"You know," he continued, "so they don't end up like you?"

I felt the skin over the surface of my stomach tighten. And though I knew that it was impossible, I felt a very slight little *kick* at the base of my gut.

Too early, I thought. *Much too early.*

The thing inside of me couldn't have been much larger than a pea.

I looked back at Carl, who was already making his way off in the direction of the booth, ready to buy us a ticket on the ride. But I managed to reach out and catch hold of the sleeve of his shirt. I pulled him back.

His expression was full of surprise—*outrage*—and I thought to myself then about how much I hated it. About how much I couldn't *stand* those dumb, little school-boy expressions of his. He was a grown man—twenty-three—for *God's sake*. But, then again, why'd I gone and allowed an overgrown school boy to knock me up in the first place was the million-pound question . . . and one which plagued me for the longest time.

The answer, though, was obvious all along.

Staring me in the face.

Fear.

"Shut up," I said.

And then Carl gave me another of those oh-so-innocent expressions: one of those ones with the pursed lips and the flushed-out eyes. I tried my best not to throttle him, but it did take more than a little bit of self-restraint.

"You wanna go on the ride or not?" Carl said, his voice sounding much sterner than before.

Though I knew that I really *didn't* want to take the ride, at the same time I knew that I was curious to see just what it was that had shaken up that pair of kids who'd got off.

"Hey there, folks!" the man in the tux said.

This broke Carl's concentration on me, and he turned to look at the man. "How much?" he said.

The man gave him a price, and Carl shuffled a few coins about his pocket and then tipped them out into the man's hand. Though I could see that the standard procedure was for the customer to pay at the booth beside the ride, the man in the tux—maybe because it was a quiet night at the fair—took Carl's change from him and slid it beneath the opening in the glass window there. The person snuggled within the booth slipped back a pair of papery tickets to the man in the tux, who, in turn, handed them to us.

With drawn-back lips, a revolting smile, Carl handed me my ticket. "Now don't you lose that, okay?"

I rolled my eyes at him, but soon found myself more distracted by the man in the tux opening up the door to the cart. He smiled all over the place as he watched us take up our seats within. With us sat inside, he said, "Okay, folks, have a good ride!"

That too-happy hop to the man's voice, I thought, would follow me about for days, echoing about my skull.

What I didn't know, though, was that, just as soon as I got through with the ride, I would've forgotten all about such a minor detail as the man in the tux's voice.

3

JUST LIKE PRETTY MUCH any other haunted house ride, the cart ground its way over the unoiled rails. Inside of the place it smelled a lot of furniture polish, and I could feel the stink of it making my nostril hair itch. I still had a bit of a bloody taste in my mouth from biting my lip back outside the ride.

As the cart trundled onwards, ploughing through the darkness, I wondered just what the fuss had been about. Everything around us was pitch black. The only light I could see at all came from where the fading daylight snuck in through the gaps in the walls of the ride.

When I slipped a glance at Carl, he gave me a shrug.

I guessed that our little argument outside the ride had been forgotten for a few moments.

We passed on through another set of transparent plastic flaps which hung down from the doorway, and into yet more darkness.

I heard a slight noise at the back of Carl's throat, as if he was just about to say something when, out there, in the darkness, I *did* see something.

Nothing more than a slight sparkle. Nothing more than a *glimmer* of light.

I stared harder at it, tried to make it out.

But I failed.

There just wasn't enough lighting in this place.

The cart ground to a stop. I forgot that I'd already dug my teeth into my lip earlier and I did it again. A fresh flash of pain passed through me. As I continued to stare out, at that glimmer, trying to make sense of it, I felt Carl's hand grip hold of my thigh. I brought my hand up, ready to give him a smack, but it was right then when the lights came on.

Cages. All around us. Wall to wall.

Stacked one on top of the other.

I felt my chest tighten even more.

The bright light was blinding.

At first, in that *brief* flash, I couldn't make sense of it.

And then, sooner than I could gather, the lights all went down again.

The cart sprang back into life.

Its wheels ground along the track, drawing us back out, through the darkness.

And, just like that, we were back out again.

Outside the ride.

It wasn't till the man in the tux was undoing the lock on the cart that I turned to Carl and said, "Did you see them?"

"See what?" he said.

"The children," I said. "In the cages—all of them looking out at us?"

Carl just gave a shrug. He jutted his lip out in a pout. Then, apparently feeling like he needed to act the gentleman right now, he helped me down from the cart. "Couldn't see nothing," he said, finally, "It was all dark."

As we walked away from *Surprise, Surprise!* I was of half a mind to turn around and take the ride again—to make sure that I'd seen what I *thought* I'd seen. But then I felt another kick at the base of my gut . . . that kick I knew *couldn't* be the child growing inside of me, not yet . . . and yet I was so sure there *was* a kick.

4

I T WASN'T TILL a week later when I found out and, by then, the summer fair had left town.

I'd been coming back from my job at the local supermarket, where I'd been working the till. My feet were killing me. It felt like somebody had stabbed a whole bunch of pins directly into my soles. It was just after I'd pulled out some milk from the fridge, poured it out over a whole bowl of cereal and taken a bite that I noticed the newspaper lying rolled up on our kitchen table.

Though I don't usually bother to so much as glance at the free newspaper that comes through our letterbox, that day there was something which seemed to compel me to.

The newspaper had got half stuck in the letterbox when it had been delivered and it was now soaked on one side from the rain that'd fallen down.

I sat down at the kitchen table, bowl of cereal before me, and the taste of dried strawberries and milk on my tongue. With my free hand, the hand which didn't hold the spoon, I flipped the paper over and glanced over the headline story.

Girl missing for a week

I looked to the photo attached to the article, saw her dressed up there in her school uniform. The girl was kind of chubby, with tangled, black hair. She gave the camera one of those half smiles— one of those *self-conscious* smiles.

I couldn't help thinking that the girl reminded me of how I'd been myself at that age.

I read through the details, while waiting out, with half an ear, for any sound of Carl's van droning up and parking at the side of the street outside.

The girl, I soon found out from the report, had gone missing back at the summer fair. That she'd been walking around with her parents when she'd just *disappeared*. Nobody had seen her since.

It was then that I leaned back on the hard-backed chair I sat on and thought again about that ride, about *Surprise, Surprise!*

In all honesty, I had attempted to put it out of my mind, and, it seemed, I'd succeeded in doing so till that moment, with the paper before me and my worst fears, my worst *observations*, of the summer fair playing out on my mind.

Could what I saw there, at *Surprise, Surprise!* have had something to do with this girl's disappearance?

I did think about going to the police, about telling them what I'd seen, but it was only when Carl returned home from work, with that sleepy, sloppy grin of his, and I told him just what I thought that he dismissed it right out of hand.

Told me that I was just *making stuff up*.

And so, not wanting to waste police time, I tossed the damp newspaper in the bin and forgot all about it.

5

I GUESS THE YEAR that followed could loosely be defined as *hell*.

Hell because of Carl leaving . . . or me throwing him out . . . and *hell* because of the baby being born and me having to look after him without so much as a whiff of his father.

One thing can be said about Carl, and that's that he's a man who believes in a clean break. Doesn't want to dwell on the past . . . no matter how much the past might dwell on him.

One of the positives of him leaving, though, one thing that I hadn't considered previously, was that at least I wouldn't find myself dragged along to the summer fair that year.

There'd be nothing at all forcing me to go.

I was getting little Paulie dressed up to be ready to go to his child-minder when I saw the newspaper which had slipped through the letterbox the day before, and which still lay on the carpet. I guess I was a little slack about picking stuff up off the floor—Paulie took up just about every second of my waking time that I wasn't working.

On the front page of the paper was a picture of that girl, the one from the year before, the one who had gone missing. They were doing a yearly follow-up. I looked over her photograph again, the one of her in her school uniform—the same one as the year before. And I caught that shimmer through my blood again, that faint feeling of recognition.

I brushed the feeling off and set my mind to the day ahead.

I had stuff to do—I needed to get Paulie to his minder, and I had to get myself to work.

So, I snatched the paper up and then deposited it in the bin.

And I thought that would be all there was to it.

It was only about an hour later, when I stood up at the checkout at the supermarket, that I thought about the paper half sticking out of the kitchen bin back home. And my mind turned to the photograph of the girl on the front cover. Something about her, it was more than familiar, more than a simple recollection—that simple *recognition*—that I had been similar myself as a school girl. There was more to it . . . in fact, and, as I scooped out a handful of change from the till drawer, I knew it instinctively.

It was a solid memory.

A *real* recognition.

6

I FLOATED ALONG for the rest of the work day, a fact which my boss—Neil—noticed. And, thinking that I maybe had a head cold, he sent me home early. Letting me leave at four rather than my regular leaving time of six.

I gave him a slightly giddy smile, and then went off to collect my things from the lockers. It was while I was bobbing about there, fetching my handbag, and my coat, that I thought about whether or not the *Surprise, Surprise!* ride might've rolled into town.

I had a couple of hours before I would have to pick up Paulie, so I figured that I might as well follow what my gut was telling me. Maybe if I went there and found nothing at all, my brain would leave the whole thing alone. Stop tormenting me.

As I trotted along the pavement, in the direction of the summer fair, I could already hear the tinny music from the crackling speakers. I gave my minty gum another couple of good chews and then rolled it into a ball and dropped it into a bin as I passed by.

For some reason, I could taste that blood in my mouth again, the blood which'd seeped out from my lower lip when I'd dug my teeth in.

As I turned the corner and caught a whiff of the buttered popcorn and the candy floss, I felt sick to the stomach. I wondered if Neil had noticed something which had passed me by. If he'd seen that I'd looked a little green about the gills.

I tried to put that out of my mind.

I had something far more urgent to see to.

I felt that same, familiar creeping autumn breeze blowing against my skin, sending a thrill through my blood, and seeming to give me a little kick.

Keeping me awake and aware.

I wandered about the fairground for maybe five or ten minutes before I came across the ride. *Surprise Surprise!* The man in the tuxedo standing up there, helping a couple out of the cart. I picked up speed, and felt my heart beating hard against my throat.

I guess that the man in the tuxedo saw me coming, because he smiled all the wider, almost as if he wanted to welcome me into his open arms. For some reason, I caught the dizzy feeling in my brain that he was some long-lost uncle of mine and that he was just about to announce the secret which he had held within himself for so many years.

As I closed on him, I found my eyes tracking onto the cart, and I knew that there was no alternative.

When I handed the coins to the man in the tuxedo, I wasn't sure at all whether or not he recognised me from the last year.

Why *would* he have?

He must've seen a huge amount of people since then.

At least he gave me no sign of recognition aside from that professional smile of his.

I got into the cart, and braced myself.

As I felt the bar come down across my lap, I felt a fizzling sensation through my veins. What would happen if I *did* see the missing girl here? What if she was staring out from behind the bars of one of the cages? What would it change exactly?

I really had no way of knowing—none whatsoever.

And there was no turning back now.

The car churned its way along its rails, and towards the plastic flaps dangling down from the entrance.

7

INSIDE, I caught that same smell of overpowering polish. When I breathed in it almost felt like somebody had dunked a rag in the stuff and then pressed it over my mouth and nose. I could almost feel the coolness of it up against my lips and cheeks. The bar which pinned me into the cart felt like an almost unbearable weight across my lap.

The darkness poured over me, like a rising tide, and I stared into the black, trying to find that glimmer I had seen before. That reflection of light on, what I'd come to realise, had been a child's eye. But, this time, there was nothing at all to see.

Only darkness.

The cart came to a stop.

I braced myself, clung tight onto the restraining bar.

Felt the muscles in my fingers all lock tight.

My heart beat against the underside of my tongue.

It was now . . . *now* the lights would blink back on.

I waited longer and longer, waited for the light to come.

And then, finally, it did.

Cages.

All of them empty.

Nothing within them.

Nothing hidden.

And, just as quickly as the lights had blinked on, they blinked back off again.

With a jerk, the cart trundled on, back on its course, headed for the exit.

8

PASSING BACK THROUGH the crowds at the fairground, I felt numb, like the autumnal chill no longer made a mark on me—didn't so much as cause me to shudder.

I had to get away from the grinding music, from the constant calls from the people at the various games, and attractions. Away from the too-strong scent of the buttered popcorn and candy floss. It wasn't difficult. The fairground did not pull at me. It did not snatch at my heels like a creeping tar with a mind of its own.

It released me.

When I got to the child-minder's house, I'd pretty much put the whole ordeal at the fairground out of my mind.

What was the point in thinking it over anymore?

I'd gone into the place once more—into *Surprise, Surprise!*—and I had seen nothing, nothing but the emptied cages all of them standing there, on either side.

No children.

It was while I stood on the doorstep, staring into the frosted glass that I felt a real chill creeping up my spine. All of a sudden, a queasiness seized hold of my stomach. I warded it off and then something told me *not* to knock, that I *shouldn't* knock.

And so I reached down, for the doorknob, and I turned it.

Inside, the house smelled like it always did, of damp and fish guts and mould.

I wished that I could afford another child-minder, but it seemed that while I tended to the checkout, that simply wouldn't be a possibility. Leaving Paulie with this woman, in this squalid pit she called a home, was the only option I had for the time being . . . that or me quitting my job to stay and look after Paulie, with both of us starving.

I took one step—two steps—into the house, and immediately I

knew that nobody was home. That the whole place was deserted. I reached for the light switch and an exposed, bare bulb blinked on above my head. It chased the shadows into the corners. I tried to keep my breathing shallow so as not to take that fish-gut stench too far down into my lungs.

After I'd searched the kitchen, and the sitting room, and then the bedroom and study upstairs, I found nothing at all.

No note.

No nothing.

I fled the house as soon as I could—I returned home with the vague notion that my child-minder might've dropped Paulie off early. Maybe left him with one of the neighbours. But when I got to knocking on doors, there was no reply. Nothing at all.

Paulie, and the child-minder, it seemed, were both gone.

9

THE POLICE LISTENED to me patiently—but of course they did, it *was* their job after all.

And they told me, even more patiently, that they'd look into the matter, but if there was no sign of the child-minder, or my baby, then they could only ask questions. Do their best.

But I didn't want them to do their 'best,' I wanted them to bring my baby back.

I continued going to work, there was nothing else for me to do, not unless I wanted to get myself turfed out of the small flat where I lived with Paulie. There was no news on Paulie, or the child-minder, though I did go over to the house several times after work and knock on the door, interrogate the neighbours. Nobody seemed to know anything.

The final day of the summer fair snuck on me, and I found my mind slipping away from me while I was at work. Several times I gave people the wrong change, only to have them frowning at me, and either handing back the extra pennies, or demanding that I make up the difference. When I got off that day, I almost ran all the way to the fair, knowing where I had to head.

At the *Surprise, Surprise!* ride, I found the same man in the tux standing there, helping people in and out of the cart. This time when he saw me, though, the smile slipped off his mouth, and his eyes left mine as if he might be able to pretend he had never even seen me.

"Hey!" I said, as the man in the tux tried to duck out of the way, to some hidden spot down the side of the ride.

Reluctantly, the man glanced back over his shoulder at me. "Yes?" he said, the faintest of smiles lining his lips.

I strode right up to him, so that I was only about a nose length from his face. I could smell his mouldy stench of cologne, mixed in with halitosis. "I want to see," I said.

He raised his eyebrows.

"In there," I said, pointing to where the cart with a fresh pair of teenagers had just disappeared through the doorway. "I want to see what you've got in there—with all the lights up."

The man gave me a sly smile and then turned away, attempting to escape. "You'll have to pay admission," he said.

A flash of pain passed through me. I felt it tug at my heart. Burrow deep into my chest. I reached out and grabbed a hold of the lapel of his tuxedo and then I stared hard into his dark blue eyes. Through gritted teeth, I said, "You. Take. Me. In. There. *Now!*"

He wilted.

10

W E WAITED until the latest cart had emerged from within the ride.

The kids—just like everybody I'd observed who'd passed through *Surprise, Surprise!*—emerged blinking in the fading evening light. Looks of confusion spread across their faces.

The man in the tuxedo, with a grim expression, reached behind the ticket booth and he produced a sign which read 'Out of Order.' He hung the chain of the sign up over the doorway to the ride, to the cart track which disappeared within.

He led me in through those plastic flaps dangling down.

As we walked inside, the lights steadily blinked on.

I felt myself dazed for several moments.

Blotchy, purple-blue spots appeared on my vision.

I kept my eyes fixed on the heels of the man walking before me —I couldn't take my eyes off him, couldn't trust him, not for *one* second.

When we reached the chamber where the cart would stop, now fully illuminated, I looked about the place, saw that it was empty. That there was nothing there. Not even so much as the cages which I'd seen previously.

The man in the tux turned to look at me, his expression grim, and his eyes with a dead quality to them. I pondered that this was maybe akin to a magician being forced to reveal his trick—to peel back the mystery and show just how mundane the reality was.

"In here," he said, "you see just what you *wish* to see."

I looked about some more, still unsure whether or not I could trust that the man in the tux hadn't *somehow* concealed something of the surroundings.

But I *couldn't* see anything else.

Just blank, grey plasterboard walls.

No children.

Not even any cages.

Nothing for me to see.

The man turned back to me. "That is the trick of the ride," he said, even more glumly, as if I might need this potted explanation to *fully* satisfy my curiosity.

I continued to look about myself.

The man said, "May I be so impertinent as to ask just what you saw exactly?"

For a couple of heartbeats, I was reluctant to answer, but then I decided that I must, that—really—there was no other option.

"Children," I said. "Children inside cages."

The man in the tux gave a slight nod, and then he glanced about the empty room. "The mind," he said, "It plays tricks on every one of us. It can *intimidate*, it can frighten, and it can lead us into madness if we allow it."

"Yes," I said, my tone now deadpan.

We stood there for what might've been another five minutes and then the man in the tux led me out of the ride. With a doleful nod, he wished me well, and I headed off back home.

Three days later—three days after the fair left town—I got a call from the police telling me that they'd managed to intercept my child-minder, down at a southern port. She had my baby—my *Paulie* —and, other than being a little ill-tempered, he was well.

Later that evening, in a police car, Paulie returned to me.

I thanked the police officers what must've been about a thousand times, offered them cup after cup of tea, and apologised about the lack of food I had in the house.

When they finally left, I couldn't keep myself from bursting out into tears, from simply breaking down, Paulie clutched to my chest, and sinking to my knees on the kitchen floor. Paulie cried too. And we stayed like that for the longest time.

After that day life went back to normal. I worked out an

arrangement with one of my neighbours—a stay-at-home mother with two kids of her own. She was sympathetic to my situation, to what had happened to me. The story had been all over the news.

I went to work every day, like normal, and each day, without fail, I would scan the headlines of the local newspaper, and then, on my fifteen-minute morning coffee break, flip through the pages trying to catch a mention of the name of the girl who'd disappeared.

They never found her.

RANDOM ACTS OF
SILENCE

Many Voices, One Face

JULIAN could see him every morning.

Looking back at him from the bathroom mirror.

He saw him while he was shaving, while he was sat on the toilet with his quarter-folded newspaper, while he was brushing his teeth.

Every morning.

Without fail.

There.

In the mirror.

Though he had observed him there, for what must've been a week now, Julian really hadn't bucked up the courage to have a proper look.

Because, really, there was something deeply *suspect* about one chap looking another chap in the eye in a bathroom . . . even if said chap was, most probably, a figment of imagination.

To be honest, more than anything else, Julian wanted him to go away.

All that changed, however, a day later while—just like normal— Julian was brushing his teeth, his tie swinging down from the neck of his white *work* shirt, and threatening to swoop on into the constantly flowing stream of water coming out of the tap.

Like normal, Julian replaced his toothbrush in its porcelain holder, and he reached out for the hand towels, which he used to dab away the toothpaste residue from his mouth.

That done, he made to turn the scuffed-up, brass handle of the bathroom door.

With a *tinkle* of some dainty thing breaking loose from within the mechanism, the handle came off in his hand.

He blinked a couple of times at the handle, then looked back to the door, to the perfectly round hole where the handle had only just now rested.

Bright white daylight beamed in through the gap.

He crouched down at the door, made a hook of sorts with his fingers and then poked them through the gap. He gripped the other side and tugged hard.

No movement whatsoever.

He looked back to the handle, knowing that it was one of those with a push-button lock. The button on the handle, the handle that he now held in his hand, was still depressed inwards and he knew, whatever it was that made the lock actually work—it might've been gremlins for all he knew—had got itself stuck, and, by extension, Julian was *also* stuck.

He considered his options.

The first which occurred to him was to break the bathroom door down—by far the *easiest* option . . . though one which might well result in him losing his deposit for the house when he moved out later in the summer.

He glanced to his wristwatch—the golden one with the shiny hands that he'd inherited from his father.

If he managed to get out *right now* then he would arrive to his meeting on time.

But, if he dwindled here for half an hour—or, God help him, *more*—then he would almost certainly miss it.

Over his shoulder, the other clear option was the window.

But, what with the quirks of this being a Victorian house, and with inside bathrooms having been a novelty for a great part of the nineteenth century, it had been tacked onto the attic—the third floor up from ground level.

Julian supposed that he *could* shimmer on down the drainpipe outside . . . but, then again, he'd never been the best climber so that might well be a rather rash judgement.

So, the door it was then.

144

Deposit be damned.

Julian backed up to the other side of the bathroom. As he made his way over to the window, he found that he had to duck down so as not to bang his head on the incline of the roof above. He glanced out through the frosted glass of the bathroom window, only just about absorbing the blurry shapes of the moving pedestrians and cars outside.

The world that he needed to get back to as soon as he could.

Or more quickly . . . if possible.

And so, like the proverbial bull, Julian hunched his shoulders and ran flat out at the door.

APPROXIMATELY two seconds later, Julian found himself on a heap on the floor.

His shoulder, more than anything else, ached terribly.

He had attempted to shoulder charge the door, but to not avail.

As he blinked away the waves of pain which flushed their way up his spine, he noted how not so much as a fleck of paint had been disturbed by his charge.

He drew in a deep breath.

Checked his watch again.

Even though he knew that, really, no time at all had passed.

He breathed out the deep breath.

Tried to get that fizzling sensation out of his blood.

He could feel himself sweating, that unpleasant prickling feeling, and he got the feeling that, if he continued to exert himself in the same fashion, for any extended period of time, then he would end up having to take another shower.

As he sat there, on the seat of his trousers, trying to work out his next plan of attack on the bathroom door, he heard one of those comical, "*Psst!*" sounds coming from above his head.

Coming from the bathroom mirror.

Julian blinked a couple of times, hoping that might clear this aural delusion he was having, but . . . no luck.

"*Psst!*"

Julian held firm another heartbeat, and then, feeling like something was weighing his shoulders down, he reluctantly swivelled his neck upwards to look at the bathroom mirror.

There he was.

A balding man.

He must've been sixty, maybe seventy, Julian wasn't very good at telling ages.

Despite the leathery wrinkles spread all over his face, inset into his forehead, and around his eyes, the goatee which sprouted from his chin was jet black, and looked very well nourished. The hair which remained, collected about the man's ears, and which stood up in a pair of symmetrical tufts at either side of his scalp, was also that same *jet* black.

Julian vaguely hoped that he might look so virile at that age . . . whatever age it was . . .

The man had no body to speak of, and his head appeared to be —for want of a better phrase—*floating in space.*

Or, if Julian really wanted to get technical about it, *disembodied.*

Julian looked the man in his chocolate-brown eyes—*kind* eyes, and he tried to get his thoughts straight, tried not to think too hard about what it was that he was witnessing right here, and right now.

"Trying to get out?" the man said.

Julian held himself still, tried not to show the man that he was trembling, and then he gave a gentle nod.

"Aye," the man said, "I've been trying to get outta here for *years.*"

The man seemed a touch dejected about this and, Julian supposed, that was fair enough given that if he himself had been trapped in this bathroom for years he'd probably feel the same.

Though Julian knew that he would sound like a total idiot, he decided that he might as well ask the question. "Do you, uh, know how I can get out of here?"

The man pressed his lips together tightly in a way that, to Julian, might've seemed like he was working out whether or not he should trust him with the answer.

But why should escaping from this bathroom be such a riddle?

The man eyed Julian closely. "Not been taking your pills —have ye?"

Julian felt his heart well in his throat, for a couple of seconds it was difficult, if not impossible to speak. He could feel that old familiar aching down deep in his stomach, and he knew that, if he didn't watch himself, he would burst out into tears.

"I've . . . I've been *trying* to give them up," Julian said.

The man again pressed his lips together. "Hmm, and against doctor's orders, huh?"

Julian looked away from the mirror. He didn't want to face up to him. Why did he have to answer him at all? . . . Why was he making it so that he needed to be accountable to a *delusion?* . . .

Because that was just what he knew it was . . . he had rationalised it for himself, with the aid of a dozen or more psychiatrists throughout the years . . . and yet . . . and yet . . . he just couldn't make himself believe that it *wasn't* there . . .

Julian finally found his voice. "Yes," he said. "Against doctor's orders."

The man in the mirror tutted to himself for what seemed, to Julian, like an awfully long time. It reminded Julian of an old school-master he'd once had, one of those who would never need to raise his voice to silence a class, he only ever needed to look *disappointed.*

But why should this delusion be *disappointed* in him?

After all, this delusion was *part* of him.

Was Julian so fatally self-destructive?

. . . That was another of those psychiatric terms . . .

"Shoulda taken the pills, Jules," the old man said.

"Huh?" Julian said, fixing his stare on his very brightly polished brown shoes.

He had made such an effort today, had wanted to look his immaculate best. Just as he had every single day since his release. And he had been doing so well, for more than a year now. In fact, he was quite certain that nobody at the office had so much as a clue that they were working with an ex-nutcase.

But now, these past few weeks, *today*, all of that had changed.

And all he'd wanted to do was experiment—*prove* something to himself.

Prove to himself that he *could* do it . . . that he could make it just fine without taking those pills of his . . . and now look at him, trapped in a bathroom with one of his own delusions . . . and, to top it all off, with an aching shoulder *too*.

"Jules?"

Julian looked back up to the mirror, to the man there.

He was smiling now.

That was how these delusions always ended up—with *smiling*.

Julian couldn't help but smile back.

As if they were sharing a sort of joke between the two of them.

A *silent* joke.

Something that only the two of them could understand.

The Tick Of The Tock

B Y HIS WATCH, Julian spent another hour in the bathroom.
He made another seven attempts to barge on through the door, but he had a success rate of precisely zero percent.

And he was sweating worse than ever now.

He could feel it dampening the back of his shirt.

Yes, siree, one thing was for sure, if he *did* actually manage to get himself out of the bathroom, he would, at the very least, need to give himself a hot shower before he dared set foot across the threshold, before he headed off to work.

There was no way that he would arrive to the meeting on time now . . . no *way* in hell.

And yet Julian found that strangely relaxing.

Like it was one thing that he no longer needed to worry about at all.

He couldn't change it . . . *he* couldn't travel backwards in time . . . could he?

With a thick *slap!* Julian smacked his temple with his open palm.

He felt the pain sting, seep right down to his skull.

He had got that *straight* ages ago, that he couldn't travel backwards in time.

Who had it been with?

Doctor Mellows?

Or Doctor Sanchez.

Had it been Doctor Paulsen?

His mind skipped like a scratched-up record to think about it . . . or should that have been like a scratched-up hard disk? After all, that was all that he did all day, spent his time skirting about hard disks. Dragging this file here. That file there. And *la-di-da-di-DAH!*

That was the song he would sometimes sing to himself as he sat there, clicking his mouse, flurrying his fingers over the keys.

Snapping numbers into columns, ordering letters alphabetically, scouting out shapes, making sense of all, assigning roles.

Work, work, work.

That was what it was.

Work.

Julian blinked a couple of times. Tried to get himself shot of those thoughts. When those thoughts descended on him it was like he was dealing with a dense fog. A dense fog which kept him trapped. Which separated him from the world . . . from the *real* world.

He hadn't felt that fog for a while, not since he'd been taking his pills.

And he'd thought that he would get along *so fine . . . superfine!*

But look at him now.

Sitting here, all soused-out, or whatever he was, and with this man staring down at him from the mirror as he sat slumped up against the toilet, his head leaning against the wall, with the faintest of *faint* smiles across his lips.

This wasn't him.

This wasn't *really* him.

This wasn't *dignified!*

He recalled one of his psychiatrists: Doctor Rayjay, Doctor Toot-a-Toot . . . Doctor *Moon?*

It'd been one of those, one of those who had always talked to him about 'dignity' about how the whole purpose their sessions together was to achieve some higher purpose, some greater sense of existence . . . to obtain *dignity.*

Well, one thing was for certain, Julian felt a *long fucking way* from dignified right now, sitting down here, on the wooden planks of the bathroom floor, stained with who-knew-how-many quantities of piss and shit and puke, and whatever else, from all the years of people living here.

It was only as Julian flexed his head back, *tilted* his head back, took in the bathroom one more time, that he noticed the man hanging from the ceiling from the end of a rope.

The Hanged Man

CREAK, CREAK, CREAK, went the rope of the man hanging above.

Julian knew it wasn't happening, but that didn't make the smell of rotting flesh any less pungent. It didn't make that sour taste at the back of his mouth any less prevalent. It didn't stop his skin from breaking out into a hundred thousand little pimples.

He looked to the man, a man dressed in brown rags, a man with a deep-blue shade to his skin. And a wicked—*wicked*—smile peeling back his lips. His open mouth hinted at the jaundice-yellow teeth within.

All this—*all this*—would've been so, so much easier to take if it hadn't been for the man in the mirror. The man who *continued* to look out at Julian. The man who wore a slight smile, and who looked like he had laughed long and hard in his life.

A *merry* man.

An infinitely *happy* man.

A man so completely unlike Julian.

Julian pressed himself up against the porcelain base of the toilet, feeling its cool surface through the thin material of his shirt. He hunched his knees up to his chest, and then wrapped his arms about them, squeezing them tight, as if rolling himself up into a ball—like some startled hedgehog—would really help him out.

But, as it happened, it made him feel a little better.

It made his pulse sound in his ears.

What was it that he had read about the importance of the heart-beat, of hearing *one's own* heartbeat?

Did it have something to do with his mother?

Julian couldn't help but bare his teeth at *that* thought. All those doctors—all those *psychiatrists*—they had to bring his mother into everything.

153

Oh, they had asked *so* much!

In his mind, Julian could hear their nagging, *whining* tones:

What did your mother do for a living, Julian?
What's your first memory of your mother, Julian?
When did you last see your mother, Julian?

Those questions—those *mounted* questions—well, they seemed just enough to justify him ripping out the throat of whichever psychiatrist happened to ask him once more.

But Julian had also known that there was nothing—*truly nothing*—that he could do about those questions, that he had to be sat there, in his chair, to listen to those questions, that those questions, and his answers, they were the only way of him managing to achieve his liberty, his *freedom* from the institution. His means to get hold of the keys to the *real* world . . . that world which he sat in right now.

And which had him pinned *here* in this bathroom, in this *wretched* house, keeping him from his *mediocre* job . . . was it like they said, often, in the institution? That it was a Cruel World, filled with Cruel Things, and populated by Cruel People?

Julian could hardly believe it, but he couldn't deny it, when he heard that puppy-like whimper which he sourced from the back of his throat.

This was it, wasn't it?

It had finally beaten him down?

And, oh, how he wished he knew what *it* was . . .

JULIAN took to humming after he must have been trapped in the bathroom for two, going on three, hours. That was when he found it the hardest. That was when he felt like he *had* to get away . . . even if it was only to get away from his own head.

He closed his eyes, welcomed the darkness in, and that seemed to help things greatly.

That got his foremost thoughts shot of the Hanged Man, and the Man in the Mirror, for a start. But it did very little to prevent those more subtle stabs—those remembered smells, tastes, sounds . . . those, it seemed, would come up to him like icebergs, in the night, striking the hull of a ship.

No, it was like a Whack-a-Mole.

He pushed one sense away, and all the others popped *right up* before he could so much as squeeze the grip of his mallet.

And so he opened his eyes again.

They were still there.

The Hanged Man.

The Man in the Mirror.

Present. And. Correct.

He looked from those chocolate-brown eyes of the Man in the Mirror to the back of the Hanged Man as he slowly twirled away on the end of his rope, and Julian wished, more than anything else, to simply find himself out of the bathroom.

Not even necessarily at work.

In bed . . . in bed, all tucked up, that would do.

But he knew the chances of that happening were precisely zero for as long as he sat all slumped here, between toilet and wall, with these two *characters* for company . . . and those pills of his forgotten at the back of his sock drawer.

Would those pills make this all go away?

Would they make things all better?

Would it be like his mother . . . *kissing* his boo-boo all better?

He wished that he could get his mind off his mother.

That he could escape that *bitch!*

But he knew, as the psychiatrists had all told him, that she would forever be part of him, forever be inside his thoughts, stuffed away in some nook, or crevice, of his mind, ready to pop up and surprise him at the most inopportune of moments.

Like now.

Mother

JULIAN watched his mother shimmer out of thin air.

She appeared before his eyes.

Like one of those vanishing tricks that those 'magicians' would perform on afternoon television, back when he'd been a kid.

The way they would mysteriously make a car seem to *shimmer* into being in the middle of the soundstage.

Just.

Like.

That.

His mother wore a light-purple turtleneck sweater, one of those which flattened out her chest, that *large* chest which all the other kids at school would mock him about, the chest which he had drunk his first *drink* from . . . she wore the golden cross, too, about that flimsy chain, about her neck. That *thin, dainty, snapable* neck. . . no, those were the thoughts that the psychiatrists had told him *not* to use . . . the train of thought that he had been told off, time and again, for travelling down . . . and here he was, just like a runaway train, the driver long ago having thrown himself off into the bushes at the side of the tracks—*full speed ahead!*

His mother crossed her arms over her chest. She had a faint expression of disapproval.

Just how he remembered her.

Precisely how he remembered her.

He waited there, feeling his heart beating against his throat, and he wondered whether she would speak to him. If she had something *important* to tell him. He recalled, chatting with the other patients, the other patients in the institute, and how they all had their own stories of seeing their parents—their *delusions*—and all of them, every last one of them, it seemed, having some grand message to deliver.

Sometimes they came from beyond the grave.

Occasionally only from across great distances.

But they always sprang out from inside of their minds.

Just as Julian's mother sprang out from the inside of *his* mind right now.

He waited on her, waited to see whether she would say something, if she had some sort of wisdom to impart to him.

But she just stood still—*over* him.

In that stolid way of hers which made him feel like he'd done something wrong.

When Julian blinked again, she disappeared.

Julian felt a prickling sensation all over the surface of his brain, as if some air bubbles had got trapped within his skull and they were trying to burrow their way through his brain as if it might be nothing sturdier than a *sponge*.

They had little success, though, a success rate of *zero*, in fact.

Julian found himself only in the bathroom with the Man in the Mirror and the Hanged Man. He reached up to the collar of his shirt, loosened his tie a little, gave himself some space to breathe.

Everybody needs space to breathe sometimes

He could feel the cold sweats all over his body. He imagined his body as a block of ice.

And that was when the shudders began.

Ice Ice Cold

J ULIAN WAS WINTER.

And the world was summer.

There might've been some sort of a nervous agreement between those two stations, but Julian knew that it was all a matter of degrees.

Those were the bare facts.

The facts as he saw them now.

He felt the prickle of beads of sweat as he purged water from his skin.

Melting.

So fast.

So *freely*.

No way that he could stop it now!

He felt his feet slip away from him and, just like that, easy as clicking your fingers, he found himself lying on his back, staring up at the ceiling.

The Man in the Mirror and the Hanged Man were only on the periphery of his vision now. Long-forgotten. Gone from his mind.

He breathed in deeply, felt the warmth on the air begin to melt him from the inside.

Why . . . sooner or later there would be nothing left at all!

Just some discoloured puddle on the floor of the bathroom . . .

Julian felt himself spreading out, slipping his way over the wooden floor, gushing now . . . *gushing, gushing, gushing* . . . he wished, more than anything, a desire which became so intense, so *determined*, that it drove him to tears.

He wished to melt enough so that he might breach the rim of the bathtub.

Because then he might slip on down the slippery side and swirl all down the plughole.

Just as if he was regular old water!

But, it seemed, the world held even this—simplest of desires —from him.

The granting of this desire, and nothing more, would've meant the world to him.

But the world only laughed.

Julian felt his arms about him. Felt the gentle warmth of the wooden floor.

He could hear something.

Off in the distance.

Footsteps?

. . . But, *here*, in his own home?

. . . It was an impossibility.

Something that, quite simply, could not be true.

But, if it somehow was, then surely it was an invader.

Somebody who had *broken into* his home!

The Invader

THE FLOORBOARDS outside the door creaked.

Julian perked up his ears.

No mistaking it.

Footsteps.

He looked to the Man in the Mirror, to the Hanged Man.

And then he glanced back at the door as if it might reveal the secrets of the person on its other side.

He stained his hearing—listened out for any clue.

And then, just like that, light as a leaf carried on a summer's breeze, he heard, "Doctor Winston?"

A sweet, female voice.

A voice which seemed silkier than silk, which had a certain *purr* to its tone.

Which might've lit up a *fire* if it was only given both person and motive.

Julian felt a warmth pass through his veins.

What *was* that?

Recognition?

Something like that?

But recognition of *what?*

Of an invader?

"Doctor Winston? Are you in there?"

And then he noticed the fingers poking on through the circular hole where the handle had once been. Skinny, delicate fingers. With light-blue nail varnish. No wrinkles.

Fair skin.

In that moment, Julian found his voice, though, to him, it sounded strangled, almost devoid of meaning.

". . . Yes?" he said, his voice gruff.

"Are you . . . are you *trapped?*"

Julian thought to choose his words carefully. He looked to the Hanged Man, to the Man in the Mirror. And then he glanced back at the door.

"Yes," he said, finally. "I'm trapped."

There was a scuffling sound on the other side of the door.

Julian watched the door intently as if it might buck open at any given second.

There was a *thud*.

Another.

Another.

Then a *craaackk!*

The door buckled in the centre.

It splintered.

And then, gently, as if afraid of damaging Julian's sensibility, it slowly opened up to reveal the young lady standing there.

Julian felt the frown lines form in his forehead as he tried to set things straight.

As he tried to work out just what was going on here.

He felt a fresh draught blow through.

Kiss against his skin.

He breathed it in deep, and when he breathed out, he felt like he was exhaling lead.

He took in the young lady again.

Her blond hair, held in a neat bun.

Her sable skirt which just brushed the cusp of her kneecaps.

The salmon blouse which was opened just one button, only to reveal her fragile—*birdlike*—collarbone.

Her marble-blue eyes widened. "Doctor Winston," she said, a little *gasp* in her voice.

Julian attempted to get up. He reached back for the toilet. Tried to ratchet himself to his feet. And, a little wobbling aside, he mostly succeeded.

He took in the girl—his assistant—*Sandra*.

"Goodness," she said, fingers still hovering at her lips. "You look so pale."

Julian steadied himself with the wall. Reached out and pressed his palm against it. "Yes, well," he said. "I think I might've *slipped*."

"'Slipped?'" she repeated, looking about the room.

For a stomach-crunching second, Julian thought that the Hanged Man, that the Man in the Mirror, that they had *returned*.

But when he did look about him, he saw that they were gone.

Sandra looked back at him. "Some gas," she said. "I saw that some gas got loose up here this morning . . . I . . . I didn't think there was anybody about . . . I thought it would be okay."

Julian thought about what she meant by gas . . . yes, gas . . . the gas they kept up here—a *sedative*, of sorts . . . was that . . . had that been the reason, just why he'd had . . . well, had it been anything other than a *funny turn?*

When Sandra spoke again her words seemed to almost tumble right out of her, as if she felt the need to explain everything at once. "I didn't think about it, not till after the meeting, after you weren't in the meeting, that you might be up here, that you might've got into some trouble here, in the bathroom." She looked down at the floor, to where the door handle rested, and then, with a faint smile, she shook her head. "Guess the place could do with a lick of paint, amongst other things." She looked to him. "Are you feeling okay?" she said.

He fixed Sandra back in his gaze. "No, quite all right," he said. "Feeling fine."

Sandra raised a smile to him, but it didn't reach her eyes, it failed to convince. "In that case are you ready to see Mr Halmond?"

"'Mr Halmond?'" Julian repeated.

"Yes," she said, "your eleven o'clock appointment?"

Julian looked to his wristwatch. Saw that it was five minutes to eleven.

He blinked himself back to sense.

Then he managed to put on a smile. "Yes, I'm ready."

Sandra smiled back at him. This time it was a *glorious* smile. All pearl of teeth, and sparkle of eye, gloss of lip. That smile which simply seemed to make his day . . . over and over again.

Julian hung back from the doorway as Sandra padded on off along the hall, heading for the stairs, and the downstairs of the institution.

When he was quite sure she'd slipped from view, he dared a final look into the bathroom.

Just for sanity's sake.

There was nothing there, of course.

Just a mirror.

And no 'hanged' man.

Feeling a little better about the whole thing, he ventured on off along the hallway, after Sandra.

J ULIAN sat in his plumped-up armchair, the one which looked out into the rose garden—his *famed* rose garden . . . at least in his own mind.

Over the hedge which marked the periphery of the garden, he could make out the residents, all of them moving back and forth with that trudging gait of theirs. A few orderlies and nurses moved among them, dispensing pills, or offering a helping hand.

Julian breathed in the air of his office, of the rows and rows of leather-bound books on his shelves, and he sank deeper into his armchair, a fresh block of notes before him.

A *crisp, white* page.

A pair of knocks came at the door.

"Come in," he said, sliding his ballpoint pen out from between the rings of his notepad.

He clicked the nib out from the sheath of the pen.

A man dressed in striped green pyjamas—fluffy, cream slippers —rounded the door. He looked to Julian briefly, offered neither a smile nor a grimace and, with Julian's gesture, took his place on the sofa opposite.

The man—Mr Halmond—did not make himself comfortable.

He perched himself on the very edge of the sofa, and clasped his hands.

He had deep, black circles beneath his eyes, and he seemed to be focussing on a point somewhere between the tip of his nose, and the beige, well-stained, carpet.

Julian put on his smile, the one which he hoped would seem reassuring—*friendly*—and then he said, "So, Mr Halmond, I think we were talking about your mother."

ARRIVAL. DEPARTURE.

ARRIVAL

1

LOUIE TRUDGED ALONG the pavement, rucksack slung over his shoulder. His hair was ragged and his beard was scrunchy. His whole body ached and stunk of aeroplane sweat. He shifted his backpack onto his left shoulder and rounded the corner, his parents' house coming into view.

The old grey car parked out front. Hedges in the front garden overgrown. Wheelie bins stood on the curb. His heart beat faster as he crunched up the gravel path to the familiar old blue door and rapped smartly.

No answer.

He knocked again, listening for any sound within.

Nothing.

He peered upwards to his bedroom window. Someone stared back at him. A chill ran down his collar. He held up his hand to shield his eyes from the late-afternoon sun.

No one there. Just imagining things. He examined his watch. Six thirty. The date: Sun, 14th August. Of course. His parents would be in church. He removed a jumper from his bag, made himself comfortable on the front step and slipped into a doze.

2

TWILIGHT HAD SET IN when Louie heard shoes scuffing tarmac. Familiar voices. He got to his feet. His mother and father rounded the corner, hand in hand. A panting mop of fur skittered at their heels. A dog.

"Louie!" His mother trotted up to him, knocking him back against the old blue door.

Warmth swelled in his stomach. He swallowed back the tears and hugged her.

His father joined them, a half-smile on his lips. He ruffled Louie's hair.

Louie ducked away.

His father said, "Why didn't you tell us you were coming home, kiddo?"

"Wanted it to be a surprise."

His father broke into a grin. "It's great to have you home. How was Africa? You didn't write much."

"Nah," Louie said. "It was difficult to get organised. I was away from it all most of the time. Don't worry, though, I brought back something for each of you."

His mother's cheeks reddened as she stuck the key in the door. "Oh, presents. I am excited!"

Louie examined his father, thinking that he'd got thin. "At church, were you?"

"No, just walking the dog." His father's eyes slipped from Louie's. "We don't go to *church* anymore."

The way his father spat 'church' sent a shiver down Louie's spine. Having teased his mother and father for years over their unwavering belief in a little bearded man in the sky, he was relieved they had finally seen sense. He resolved to let it pass for now, to enjoy his home-coming.

Gloating could wait.

The dog jigged around his feet. He crouched down, patted it on the head and then straightened. It padded off into the kitchen. "I thought you hated dogs."

"No," his mother said. "I never said 'hated.'"

His father wrapped his arm around her shoulders. "Your old mum's coming around to new things. Only took ten years to wear her down."

His mother pouted. "Curly's only small anyway. That was one condition."

His father flashed his eyes. "And the other one was that *I* had to clean up the crap."

Louie flinched. That was the closest his father had ever come to swearing in his presence. With a yawn, he stepped onto the staircase, looking forward to a hot shower and fresh clothes. His arm brushed a black cloak draped over the banister. He screwed up his features and pinched it between his fingers, holding it up. "What's this?"

His father tugged it gently from his grip. "Use it on the early morning walks. Keeps the muggers away. Blend in with the night sky."

Louie groaned, rolling his eyes. "I can see your sense of humour doesn't improve with age."

His mother took the cloak from his father. "No, it's just a prop for the kids' autumn play. I'm still running rehearsals at the church, even if we're no longer part of the congregation."

Louie took another step up the staircase. "Right, quick shower and I'll be sociable."

"Oh, one thing, dear," his mother said. "You'll have to set up camp in the guest room."

Louie's stomach jolted. His mind felt frayed and his eyes stung. He just wanted to collapse into his bed, be surrounded by his things. "What's happened to my room?"

"You were away a long time, for years, and—"

"But it's my room! You said it would always be here."

His parents exchanged glances.

"What have you done to it?" Louie said.

His father sighed, inspected his shoes. "Turned it into a games room"

Louie's throat felt sore. "Can I at least see it?"

His father's smile disintegrated. "Maybe later."

Louie shook his head. "I can't believe you took away my room."

"Look," his father said, "I thought you would be mature about this. You're almost twenty-six. You were away for years with that damn charity. Stop being such a brat."

Louie's chest tingled. He had forgotten how infuriating his parents could be, how they could make him feel just like a child.

His mother edged closer, laid her hand on his arm. "Just for tonight. I promise tomorrow we'll sort it out. Get your things back in their places."

"Where *are* my things?"

"In the attic. I'll fetch them after you've showered."

"Okay," Louie said, realising he *was* being a brat. "Really, don't worry about it. I can cope with what I've got in my backpack for now."

His mother smiled and then, along with his father, disappeared into the kitchen.

Louie paused in the middle of the staircase, mind swimming. On the plane ride he had prepared himself for the changes that would have taken place in the house, but the idea that he no longer had his own room in the house bothered him.

3

LIKE ALWAYS, the guest room was pristine. A glass water decanter occupied a silver tray on the bedside table. He examined the virgin sheets and the springy mattress. He allowed himself a smile. It would be nice to sleep in a bed tonight after years of camp beds.

Dark orange light streamed in through the roof window, casting rays over the spotless bedspread. He leapt onto the bed, feeling a childish pleasure at putting wrinkles into tightly-drawn sheets. He allowed himself a few minutes, staring up into the darkening sky through the glass before snatching up one of the fluffy, cream towels and making for the bathroom.

Once showered, Louie spilled the contents of his rucksack onto the thick carpet and fished out a pair of cut-off jeans. He felt a familiar bulge in the pocket. His Swiss Army knife. He reached in and pulled it out. In Africa he had carried it everywhere.

He set it down on the bedside table and then reconsidered. It felt strange not to have it with him, so he returned it to his pocket. With his parents' presents crocked under his arm, he strode into the kitchen.

His mother served them leak and potato soup, and set the table with a wicker basket filled with hot bread rolls, a butter dish alongside. Louie slurped the soup, enjoying the warmth which bathed his tongue and throat. During dinner Curly slept on a ravaged purple pillow in an alcove beside the oven, his food bowl empty save a pair of tiny bones. Never had Louie encountered a dog that didn't beg at the dinner table. His father had obviously spent serious time training him.

After dinner Louie handed a present to his mother and a present to his father. They tussled with the brown paper wrapping. His mother got hers open first. An ornamental hippo, carved from mahogany. She set it on the table, gave it a stroke with her finger. "Beautiful. Thank you."

His father ripped open his, skinning the remaining wrapping paper to reveal a thick twig with brightly-coloured string wrapped around it. A few silver beads hung off strands and rattled against the wood. Wrinkles formed in his father's forehead as he examined it.

A buzz hummed through Louie, delighting in seeing his father—nature's most basic element—coming to terms with something slightly kooky.

His father cocked his head to one side, his eyes never leaving the object. He wore an expression that suggested it might leap up and slash him across the throat.

"What's the matter, Dad?"

His father's expression cleared. He smiled uneasily. "Nothing, nothing. It's fine."

"It's a white witch's wand. That's what the guy said, anyway."

He set the wand to one side and met Louie's gaze. "Thank you, son."

Louie looked to his mother for support, wanting her to tell his father it was all a joke. However, his mother also stared at the object. Louie straightened in his chair, feeling his words slurring with fatigue. "If you don't like it just chuck it out. I won't be offended. Cost almost nothing. Just wanted to wind you up. Thought you still believed in God and stuff."

His father collected up the bowls and deposited them in the sink. "I'm going to take the dog out." He crouched down. "Curly?"

Curly twitched her ears and scrabbled up.

"I'm coming too," Louie said.

His father cracked open the back door and Curly cantered out.

Louie stooped over his mother and planted a kiss on her cheek. "Thanks for dinner, Mum."

A FRESH BREEZE blew outside, rustling bushes and whistling through tree branches. Stars blinked down on them through the clear sky. Louie's breath clouded in the frigid air. Curly foraged through the garden, sniffing at plants and cocking his leg.

"I'm sorry, Dad," Louie said. "I really didn't mean to offend you. I thought twice about giving you the wand, you know, and then you said you don't go to church anymore, and I presumed you'd see the lighter side."

"I'm not offended."

Louie slipped his father a sidelong glance, unconvinced. "Why *did* you stop going to church?"

"Lots of reasons."

"Give me one."

"The same reason we started going."

Louie's blood froze. "Charlie?"

His father pressed his lips together and rubbed his eyes.

"What happened?"

"Nothing," his father said, waving his hand. "Really. It's nothing." Tears dampened his cheeks. He turned his back to Louie, called Curly and then re-entered the house.

Another shudder paralysed Louie's nerves. He stared up into the stars and lost himself in his memories of that horrific day.

5

FIFTEEN YEARS AGO, Louie, aged eleven, had been putting the finishing touches to a snowman with his three brothers out on the road. His oldest brother, Charlie, who had just turned seventeen, slotted the nose and eyes into place—a carrot and a pair of pennies—before brushing the snow from his gloves and declaring that they would head home for hot chocolate.

As they turned the corner, a group of giggling kids burst from snow-dusted bushes and pelted them with snowballs. One caught Louie right on the nose, knocking him to the ground, and, before he knew it, the children piled in on him, stuffing snow into his collar, smushing his face into the freezing tarmac. He cried out for them to stop but it only encouraged them.

When the children tired, he had looked up through blurry eyes to see Charlie standing over him, hands on belly, chortling. Louie leapt to his feet and shoved Charlie as hard as he could in the stomach. Charlie tumbled backward, slipped on the ice and cracked his head on the curb.

He recalled the blue and red ambulance lights against the pearl white snow. His parents had no capacity to reassure him. All their affection was for Charlie, their dying son. His older brothers Mike and Andy, too, were preoccupied with Charlie.

Louie had just stood back, looking on from a safe distance, trying to wriggle warmth into his numb toes.

6

LOUIE SNAPPED back to the present, wiping tears from his eyes. He found himself alone. His father had gone back inside. He returned to the kitchen to find his parents embracing. He had no intention of interrupting them so he marched through the house, up the stairs and back to the guestroom.

The world spun before his eyes. A combination of exhaustion and unwanted memory. He tucked himself into bed and rested his head on the pillow, closing his eyes and praying for sleep.

He woke in the dark, checked his watch. Just past midnight. He listened to the night-time house sounds. The whirring and clunking of the dishwasher. The sucking of pipes overhead. Whispering drifting along the corridor.

He shucked the duvet and stood. He listened more closely. Yes, he was sure. Definitely whispering. His father's voice. He approached the door. The sounds emanated from his old bedroom, the games room.

He stole out onto the landing and drew up at his old bedroom door. Yellow light trickled out around the edges. His father's voice was too low to make out. He knocked, only then noticing, in the gloom, a large, metal lock on the jamb. Dozens of punchable keys.

Inside, his father's voice fell silent. Bare feet slapped the floor-boards. His father had taken up the carpets too. Was Louie's presence so sickening to them that they had to remove every trace of him from the house?

The door opened a crack. His father's face appeared in the gap. His eyebrows rose and his lips parted. "I thought you were your mother."

"I wanted to see my room."

His father's eyes glittered for the first time in a long while. Not since Charlie had died had his expression taken on so much life. A thrill passed through Louie. All these years Louie had wanted to prove himself, to show he could more than make up for Charlie's loss. Even if it were so silly as indulging his father in a train set, a giant jigsaw puzzle or whatever he kept in the games room. The door creaked open and Louie stepped inside.

The walls were painted black. Strange symbols shone in white luminous paint. There was no furniture and Louie noticed a circle chalked onto the floor. His father stepped back and two hooded men slipped past his father and seized hold of Louie.

The world flashed. Louie's mouth and nose got a sharp whiff of something like alcohol and then everything disappeared into darkness.

DEPARTURE

1

AN ENGINE HUMMED. Louie's head felt numb. He touched his eyeballs to convince himself he was really awake. He scrabbled to get a grip, feeling himself slip to the side. Finally, he caught a soft material, rubber. The spare tyre.

He recalled another episode with his brothers. A few years after Charlie had died. They had locked him in this very boot. It had taken Louie twenty minutes to locate the catch and get out. By then his brothers had disappeared inside to play video games. Often he wondered whether they ever would have checked on him if he hadn't escaped.

In the pitch black Louie located the catch and tugged. It remained solid. Locked from the outside. Blood rushed to his brain and his cheeks flushed. He screamed out and pounded his fists against the inside of the boot.

The car slowed.

He lay still, waiting.

The car stopped. A door squealed open and footsteps sounded. A dog barked. Curly. The boot popped open and his father towered over him. Louie breathed deep, but before he could speak the damp rag pressed his nose and mouth once again.

2

A COOL BREEZE blew over Louie's sweaty face. Cramp crawled up his arms and legs. He tried to move, only to find his limbs bound. A fire crackled. Its uneven light flickered, giving off an orange glow. He moved his neck and glanced to his side, seeing his father. The two hooded men stood alongside, sharpening knives against rocks.

Louie lay on a stone table. The back of his head felt cold and ached from resting against its hard, flat surface. The stars above whirled. He wished they would stop. He closed his eyes and took deep breaths, trying to regain his composure. No way this could be happening. He squeezed his eyes shut and open several times, convinced it was a dream. That, somehow, someone had slipped something in his drink on the plane and that he might wake up, five minutes from landing.

But no, this was real.

Louie yanked at the ropes tying his arms and legs. There was some give. He gave them another tug and got a few centimetres of movement in his right arm. Eyes fixed on his father and his friends, he kept up his attempts to break free of the bindings, but it was useless. The rope would give no further.

He worked his fingers along the pocket of his cut-offs. His neck strained as he tried to get a better look. He brushed his Swiss Army knife. It was still there! He wormed his hand back and dipped it into his pocket. He clutched the knife and withdrew it, working to unfold the saw blade.

Paws scuttled underneath him. Snuffling. He craned his neck around. Curly trundled around the bottom of the table. He paused, cocked his leg and peed. Sniffing the air, it caught a glance at him, paused and then barked.

Louie mouthed 'shut up' to the dog. He blinked back tears.

Curly considered a moment and then barked again.

Louie's father turned from his knife-sharpening, wiped the blade on the side of his jeans and then strode toward Louie.

Louie gasped as he worked at the rope with the knife, getting his right hand, the one bearing the knife, unbound. He tucked his freed arm under his body.

His father loomed over him.

Louie's brain shot a thousand thoughts a second. He tried to ignore them all, to focus on the task at hand. He squeezed his eyes tight, concentrating on staying still, waiting for the right moment. His voice trembled when he spoke. "Dad? What are you doing?"

His father's breathing hollowed. "You almost ruined everything. Bringing that white magic into our house. That wand."

"What? What are you talking about? Ruined what? It was a joke!"

"For your perhaps."

Warm tears pooled in the corners of Louie's eyes. The whole situation was just too far-fetched to even contemplate, let alone deal with. He returned his thoughts to the Swiss Army knife. He had to escape. "Look, I said I'm sorry."

"Sorry for what?"

"The wand! What else?"

His father produced a knife. He held it up. Moonbeams glimmered along its blade. "You aren't sorry about Charlie?"

"Charlie? Of course I am. Do you think a single day goes by when I'm not sorry?"

"If you're truly sorry for Charlie then you will allow me to do this."

"What? Fucking cut me open, sacrifice me?"

His father winced. "Please, don't swear. Those words affect the energy."

"Don't talk to me about energy."

His father ran his thumb along the knife edge and then called out to the hooded men. They picked up a pair of items and approached the table. One of the men laid an item down, Charlie's battered stuffed elephant. The other placed a locket which contained a clipping of Charlie's blond hair.

"Dad! This isn't going to work. Charlie is dead!"

"But this will bring him back. We shall reincarnate him in your body."

Louie crunched his fingers into fists. It took all his mental strength to stay still, telling himself that he had to bide his time. If all three of them attacked him he would have no hope. Louie's throat dried. "But . . . But Mum. What about her? What does she say?"

"She knows."

"Why me? Why not Mike or Andy?"

"You are the one who's responsible. All of us together, sleeping in the circle, praying to Him."

"Who?"

"The Devil."

Louie spat the air from his lungs.

His father crouched down. There was a sports bag at the foot of the table. He rummaged through it and produced a black cloak which he pulled on over his head and then fumbled into place. The same black cloak which Louie had touched on the banister.

Louie jerked his right arm out from underneath him and cut the rope loose from his left. The hooded men descended on him, snatching hold of his arms. He kicked one, sending him tumbling backward and head butted the other. He cut away the rope tying his feet and the Swiss Army knife slipped from his grasp. Not daring to retrieve it, he dived off the table and sprinted away, twisting and turning until he had lost his pursuers.

3

THE HUMID SUMMER night air turned chilly around dawn. Louie clasped his arms to his chest, trying to stay warm. His bare feet felt like blocks of ice. Light flooded the area but he encountered no useful signposts, pacing on along aimlessly through country lanes. His only wish was to wake up, in the guestroom bed, and to discover this had all been a dream.

At every tiny sound, he stopped dead and scoured the area, afraid his father and the hooded men would be just behind, ready to take him back to that table. He hoped to find a house, somewhere to call the police, but the whole area seemed deserted. He had all but given up hope when he felt a tremor passing through the ground. It graduated into the purr of an engine.

Not his father's car. Not powerful enough.

A lime-green hatchback rolled over the hill.

Louie stuck out his hand and then, when it barrelled on, he stepped out into the road. It screeched to a stop. He bashed his fists on the bonnet. "Please! Please! You've got to help me! I need to get to the police!"

An elderly lady with faint blue-grey hair and watery green eyes peered out from behind the windscreen. She wore thick, plastic-framed glasses which magnified her eyeballs.

Afraid he might have scared her to death, he stepped back from the car, shouting to be heard through the car windows. "You don't need to drive me anywhere! Have you got a mobile?"

The elderly lady wound her window down a crack. "Are you running away from prison?"

He half-laughed, half-cried. "No, no! Please, I just need to make a phone call."

The locks pinged open, he rounded the car and got in.

F IVE MINUTES into the journey, Louie broke into uncontrollable sobs.

The old woman peered over at him, checked all her mirrors and then brought the car to a stop. "What is it? What's the matter?" She laid her hand on his shoulder. "Tell me all about it."

"*Please*. We have to drive. Both of us are in danger."

The old woman sighed, inspected all her windows. "Look, I've lived here forty years and there's not much to worry about, I can tell you."

Louie reeled through the entire story, leaving nothing out. He watched her eyes glaze over but words continued to spill out of his mouth, snatching the breath from his lungs and sinking his stomach. He didn't care if she comprehended or believed him. It was important that she hear him.

When he finished, he worried that she might tell him to get out of the car. He wouldn't have blamed her. If a bare-footed hitchhiker had jumped into the path of his car on a country road he probably wouldn't have braked.

She stared full on into his eyes. A slight smile played on her lips. "Sounds like you've had an awful night. I'd better take you home with me."

"No, I need to go to a police station."

"No police stations around here, but I've got a phone back at the house, if that's any good."

Louie could have kissed her. "Yes, let's go now."

She stalled the car twice before they were off and running again.

5

A HOUSE POPPED UP amongst the rolling hills and endless greenery. The old woman slowed almost to a stop and turned the wheel, directing them down a narrow road. Tree branches grazed the car roof.

The woman tutted. "Need to get someone to cut those back." She continued on along the drive and then stalled the car again outside her house. "Home sweet home."

Foliage overgrew the windows and most of the front door. Louie wondered if anyone had ever worked on the garden around here. It reminded him of an old abandoned cottage he and his brothers had come across when they'd been younger. They would often climb in and out of its battered frame until the day Charlie died and their mother had forbidden them.

The old woman hobbled over slabs of concrete up to the front door.

Louie followed her into the house.

The interior was gloomy. The old woman flipped a switch and a bare light bulb shone down on them, illuminating a dusty and cobwebbed room. A scent of ginger pervaded everything.

Louie considered the lounge set, its wooden legs mouldy and fabric stretched to the point of breaking in several places, and then decided he was so exhausted from walking all night that he couldn't possibly stay standing much longer. He had to do it now. "The phone. I need the phone."

She showed him where the phone was located and he called the police.

As he waited for them to arrive, she gave him some tea and then eggs on toast, which warmed him all the way through. After he was done eating, she offered him a shower.

To his surprise, the bathroom was well-kept. He supposed the old woman living alone meant that she seldom used the sitting room, not often did she have company, and she probably only bothered to clean the places she used herself.

The shower reinvigorated him and when he stepped out, a towel around his waist, he found a pile of spare clothes waiting outside his door. A red checked shirt and a pair of chinos. Perhaps they had belonged to her husband. They fit him Louie enough.

He headed out into the house, looking for the old woman, but she was nowhere to be seen. Maybe she had gone into the garden or to fetch something from the car. He waited in the sitting room and then, when ten minutes or so had gone by, he decided to call the police again, to check they were on their way.

He plucked the receiver and held it to his ear, looking out through window at the old lady's car. No sign of the old lady there either. He dialled the police and waited. Tones purred through the speaker. Finally he got a connection.

"Emergency services. Which service do you require?"

"Police," he said, his voice shaking slightly.

A slight paused and then, "Hello? Police."

"Yes, I called about half an hour ago." He gave his name.

"We sent a car out when you called. It should be there within the hour."

"Can't it come any faster?"

"Sir, it's a long way out there. I could send another car but it would arrive after the first."

Louie's hands shook, unable to handle sarcasm. "Okay, thank you." He latched the phone back on its hook and peered out through the window.

His father's car bucked up the drive and parked.

Louie turned to run.

The old woman appeared in his path. She sank her nails into his skin and he fell to the ground out of surprise. Blood seeped up through the wounds.

The front door clicked open and his father, with the two hooded men, bundled in. One of them brought their foot down on his chest, pinning him. His father stepped closer, bearing his knife. He glanced at the old woman. "Good of you to let us know, Minerva."

The old woman lurked on the periphery, teeth bared.

His father returned his attention to Louie. "This time we have to poke your eyes out. Just to be safe. We need to get moving, but before we do you should see who else is here."

The two men removed their hoods. Mike and Andy. Louie's brothers.

"We waited so long for you to come home," his father said.

Pain seared Louie's skull and the world blackened.

LETTING LOOSE CRAZY

A IDEN KEPPLER—of *New Street News*—steps out of his car, notepad in hand, ready for the big scoop of the day. He's been waiting for this for the last year, ever since Vincent Smith—Senior Reporter at the paper—told him about this event down here in East Nutsley, the day they affectionately term, 'Letting Loose Crazy.' He tightens his grip on the notepad and withdraws his plastic biro from the metal coil. He gives it an experimental couple of clicks and then puts pen to paper, only to see no one else around.

He furrows his brow and steps lightly along the street. There's no one about. A single paper cup drifts on the breeze, *ker-lunking* against the curb. As Aiden approaches he gives it a kick then he shifts along in the direction which he supposes to be the town square. It's just as deserted as everywhere else in this town and Aiden begins to suspect that he's having his leg pulled.

A wave of heat flushes through him because he hates it when they make fun of him, when he gets back to the paper they'll all be laughing at him, rolling about in their chairs, the evening edition forgotten. They got him all right.

Resolved not to play the fool, to head back right there and then, drive off in his car back to the office, he turns on his heel and jams his biro back into the notepad coil. He marches up the street, puffing out his cheeks as he climbs the gentle incline. And then, off in the distance, he hears a *cackle*.

His blood runs cold and he looks off over his shoulder. But there's nothing there. Nothing to see here. It's just his mind playing tricks on him, going back over those stories that bastard Vincent told him back in the newsroom. He knows just how to creep him out.

Nonetheless, Aiden increases his pace, feels a thin film of sweat break out on his forehead. Jesus, if only his fellow reporters could see him now, allowing Vincent's story to get to him, to make his spine feel like it might burst from his flesh. This whole joke—this whole thing—it seems so petty. What kind of joy might they get out of it without even seeing him panicking like this? And then he gets the feeling he's being watched.

He pivots, looks over the crimson rooftops to a hill which lurks over the whole town, like an owl ready to swoop down on its miniscule prey. Did he see some movement there? The reflection of the sun on a pair of sunglasses, or binoculars, perhaps? This is it, the setup. Of course they're all out here. Laughing their arses off at the new guy. And then a figure appears at the edge of his field of vision, at the end of the street, between him and his parked car.

There he is. One of the clowns Vincent told him about. It's a sad-looking clown, like all of them are really. His make up's all smudged, bits of flesh showing through, his peachy skin here and there. And the flower sticking out of his hat is more than wilting—it's outright dead: brown dead.

Well, this is a little different from how Vincent described it. Vincent had talked about how all the town's people, how everyone in all of East Nutsley came out of their houses to celebrate the event. But, he supposes, he might've arrived a little too early. Or too late.

Still, not wanting to lose total face with this assignment, realising that there might *actually* be an assignment, Aiden steps toward the clown, notepad clutched. "Say," he says. "Would you mind asking a few questions before the festivities begin? You know just something about what this event means to you, anything like that would be fine. I mean to say—"

The clown produces a shiny object from within its pocket. It takes Aiden approximately three seconds to twig that it's a knife. A butcher's knife. The clown cracks up in a grin.

Aiden lightens up too. "Oh, I see!" he says. "Yes, the Senior Reporter told me all about the props, that they're important in making the people afraid." He pads his jacket pocket and slips out a digital camera, which he keeps on hand. He switches it on, then says, "You wouldn't mind a quick photo? Boss is always bugging me for one so I'd like to have a bit of back up, if you know what I mean?"

The clowns remains still and makes no effort to respond. Aiden thinks there might be a slight twinkle in his eye but, other than that, there's no input into their interaction from the clown. Maybe it's all part of the show. Perhaps this clown has to keep *schtum*.

Aiden steps closer, watching the clown in the viewfinder. He takes a picture, and then another one. As he reels back through the photos he's just taken he marvels at the gleam on the blade of the butcher's knife. He glances up over the camera at the clown. "I say, that's a pretty realistic prop you've got there. Whereabouts did you track it down? Looks just like the real thing."

The clown bares his teeth, holds the knife up to his chest and says, in a gravelly voice, "That's because it *is* the 'real thing,'" and surges forward, brandishing the blade.

Aiden's heart leaps onto his tongue and he almost trips as he spins round and runs off along the street, hearing the *patter* of the clown's oversized shoes on the paving slabs behind him.

When he arrives back in the town square, he dares a look behind him. But there's no sign of the clown now. He glances round the place. Everything's deserted. Shop fronts are boarded up. No sign of life anywhere. He wonders whether the whole previous episode was some sort of a daze, because it can't really have happened. He smiles at the absurdity of it all, trying to make himself feel better. This is all it's been. Just a wind up. One long wind up. And now there only remains the matter of getting in his car and going home.

However, as he moves to double, triple back on himself, he finds that his legs are jelly. They swing from side to side beneath him. Really, that encounter, whatever it was, really took him off guard—

hit him for six. He has to actively concentrate to walk in a straight line and he finally does get a grip on himself.

He makes his way back to the street from which he just emerged and heads up to the point where he met with the clown. There's no sign of him, of course, and he rounds the corner to where his car's parked. Only to find that it's not there.

Aiden retraces his steps, looks back off down the street, wondering whether he got himself lost. But, no, it's impossible. He remembers the bent lamppost and the post box plastered in peeling, weathered advertisements. His car had been right here, not five minutes ago. He considers the prospect of car thieves in East Nutsley and dismisses it out of hand. Another, more likely, explanation might be a tow-away truck. That must be it. He's flouted some or other parking law and had his car towed off.

He slips his mobile phone out and examines the screen. It's blank. He depresses the on-off button several times, for various seconds. The thing's totally dead. Come to think of it, it feels much lighter than usual. He turns it over, slides the back cover off and sees that the battery's been removed. Now, he's certain he didn't do that. He charged the phone the night before—like always. Did . . . was there some way that the clown managed to get it off him? The clown never managed to catch up with him. One of his housemates then? It might be the sort of thing they'd do.

With a sigh, he replaces the mobile in his pocket and gazes round, wondering just what his next move will be. And then, all of a sudden, he notices a group of clowns—seven of them—standing at the top of the hill staring down at him.

Their costumes are frayed and torn, covered in dirt. They look like they've been dragged through a hedge backwards. More disturbingly, however, they all clutch a weapon. One has an axe, another a claw hammer, a scythe, secateurs, a one-armed scissor, a brick . . . and then he spots his clown, the clown from before, the one who's got the butcher's knife.

He rehashes exactly what Vincent told him would happen that morning—that he would turn up, the streets would be full of people, lots of families, and then a group of men, all dressed as clowns, would be released from a mock cage.

Vincent had said that they would rush through the town square, pulling down ladies skirts, kissing men on the lips, defecating in the streets. Aiden had to admit he'd found it all somewhat 'far out.' But Vincent had never claimed that it would be menacing—that there would be actual *weapons* involved.

The clowns eye Aiden, and he them. There's an earthy cry from one of them and they bound down toward him, arms flailing, their weapons waggling through the air. And there's nothing Aiden can do except run.

This time he does trip and fall, however, and he busts his head against the hard cobblestones. Through his dreary daze he manages to flip himself onto his back, just in time to see the clowns circle him, their heads manically cocked to one side. He holds his hands up to his face, as if they might beat him at any moment. "What?" he says. "What do you want?"

"Oh, Aidy."

That voice. It's familiar.

"You never seemed like a fast learner."

Through the makeup Aiden now recognises the facial features. The clown, the one with the knife, it's Vincent. Aiden's eyes widen. "What . . . what's this all about?"

The clown with the secateurs says, "It's something we do with all the new recruits."

Aiden recognises this clown as being the editor of the paper. Mike.

Mike continues, "It's just a silly ritual really. It's been going for a long time now. But we always do it. You could call us sticklers for tradition."

A laugh ripples between the clowns. Aiden's sure there's a note of nervous tension to it—this whole situation is just so ridiculous that he feels like he could laugh himself. But his mouth is drier than a wrung sponge in direct sunlight. "What are you going to do to me?"

"*Do* to you?" Vincent says.

"Yeah," Aiden says, feeling himself quiver, trying to tell himself that this is all one elaborate joke, that they'll let him go in a minute. Maybe someone's filming all this on a camera phone. They'll all laugh about it in the pub afterwards. He'll be buying, of course.

Vincent glances over to Mike and his fingers tighten on the knife. He looks back down at Aiden. "If only you'd done a bit better, let us chase you round for an hour or so, put up a fight. You had to show something, see? The way things are, how they've ended up I really can't see how we can let you off. You're just not what we're looking for."

"What?" Aiden says, glaring.

But there are no more words from the clowns as they bear down on Aiden, weapons bared.

SUITCASE

1

S AM LEAPT IN through the closing bus doors. He lurched
forward, grabbed the pole to steady himself, then looked
around. Three passengers, none standing. That would make it difficult to pick pockets. A battered blue suitcase in the luggage rack
caught his eye. Stickers plastered its sides from various locations
around the world: 'I Love NY,' 'I Saw The Pyramids.' He had
always wanted to travel, but he'd never got the chance.

He examined the passengers. Who was the owner? An elderly
lady wearing a fluffy hat and tweed coat gazed out the window. In
another seat, a businessman tapped away at his mobile phone. On
the other side of the aisle, a man in a leather trench coat rose and
pressed the stop button. He wrapped his fingers around the pole,
showing off a set of silver rings: all skulls and crosses, then eyeballed
Sam.

Strange bastard.

The bus decelerated then pulled to a stop. Sam shovelled his
hands underneath the bulky case and heaved it out the door. He
landed hard on the pavement, feeling the force in his knees and
lower back. No time to listen for the standard scream of: 'Stop!
Thief!' he trudged around the corner and out of sight of the
main road.

When he reached a park, he dropped the case onto a bench. His
lungs ached and he bent over double, catching his breath. Something stank. He sniffed the air, trying to locate it, then he remembered he hadn't showered this morning—they'd shut off his hot
water last week. Circumstances had pushed him to stealing, for the
moment anyway.

In the distance he thought he heard footsteps approaching. He
took off again. It wasn't far to his flat from here.

THE STEEL DOOR bounced off its rubber stopper. Several black bin liners sagged on the floor, their juices making brown puddles. Damp clawed its way up the walls and thickened the air. A yellow letter was stuck to the fridge—an overdue notification from his plumbing night course. Home Sweet Home.

Sam slid his morning bowl of cereal aside and set the suitcase on the table. He flipped the catches. They sprung open with a rusty *twang*. Unlocked. Shit. Never a good sign.

A rancid odour wormed up his nostrils. His stomach churned and he stepped back, stretching his shirt to cover his nose and mouth. A black bin liner bulged inside the case. He prodded it.

Squish.

His hopes of finding valuable contents sunk. He wiped a layer of sweat from his forehead, sniffed then decided he couldn't resist a look inside. Who knew, maybe there was cash sewed into the lining.

He snatched a pair of scissors out the kitchen drawer and made a slit. The smell turned from pungent to putrid. Bile snapped at his throat, spotting the back of his tongue. Eyes watering, he leant forward and inspected the contents. Brown mush. What in hell's name was it? He tore the hole wider. An eyeball stared back at him.

Heat rushed to his cheeks. He spewed onto the floor, then dropped to his hands and knees, retching until he had nothing left. His whole body alternated between shakes and chills. He had the get the pissing thing out of his flat.

When he'd composed himself, he put on the washing-up gloves, slapped the case shut then hauled it out the door.

In the hallway, TVs blared from behind closed doors. He cradled the case in both arms.

The electric lock on the entrance hall door groaned and Britney, one of his neighbours, stepped inside. She wore heavy eye makeup and a short black skirt. Her eyes had a shine to them which even the block of flats couldn't dull.

"Afternoon," she said. Her voice rung clear and sweet.

His stomach sank. Over time he'd nurtured various fantasies of her. They flickered over his mind, but he whisked them away. Now wasn't the time. He turned side on and squeezed past her in the skinny corridor. "Y'aight?" he said.

She sniffed. "What's that smell?" She frowned then pointed. "There's blood on your arm."

Blood was trickling out of the case, onto his skin. He prayed she hadn't noticed where it was coming from. "I—I'll take care of it in a minute."

"Don't be silly, I've got a first aid kit. Come on, I'll patch you up."

He stepped away, reaching out to disarm the lock. "It's very kind of you but—"

A fresh dollop of blood leaked from the case and splashed at their feet. Britney's eyes widened and she screamed.

He sprinted off, the case knocking against his thigh. Even several minutes from the block of flats, he heard her scream reverberate in his skull. He noticed he was heading for the main road and checked his run, jogging into a nearby side alley where he set the case down.

It would be no good dumping it. Not only would they have Britney's statement, they'd have CCTV too—him acting like a loon, running off with his arm all bloody. He had only one choice: the police.

His feet set off before his mind had fully engaged, but with every step he realised it was the right thing to do. He would ask for Brian Henderson, his parole officer, or, failing that, Officer Kite. Both of them knew him well and, for all his other failings, they knew he had no intention of getting caught up with murder, and that he was doing his best to go straight.

He plodded up the familiar stone steps and entered the police station waiting room. Blood splashed on the waxed, green floor. He quickened his pace and arrived at the reception desk, where a young male officer stood with his eyes fixed to a computer screen. "Can I help, sir?" the officer said.

"Found a suitcase."

The officer reached behind, fishing for forms stuffed into wire-framed trays. "Lost property?"

"Uh, sort of. It's got remains in it."

"Remains?"

"Yeah. Human remains."

The officer straightened, searched Sam's face then plucked the phone and dialled. He crooked the receiver between his ear and shoulder. "Stay right there."

Sam hadn't had the chance to tell the officer he wanted to deal with Kite or Brian. When he tried, the officer held up a finger and talked in hushed, hurried tones to the person on the other end.

A pair of officers appeared from a side door. Both had stern looks on their faces. One approached Sam. "This the suitcase?"

"Y—yes."

The officer bent down and inspected it. He nodded to the other. They each produced a pair of latex gloves from their pockets and carried the case between them, back where they'd come.

Sam took a step toward the exit.

A firm hand reached out and snatched his wrist. It was a middle-aged woman dressed in a grey trouser suit. "I'm Detective Linton. You're not going anywhere."

A uniformed policeman appeared at Sam's shoulder, and they marched him off down the corridor, deeper into the station. Linton held open a door and motioned for him to enter.

It was the smallest interview room he'd ever been in. None-theless, someone had managed to squeeze in chairs and a table. He sat. The uniformed officer stepped inside and stood to attention at the door. Linton locked the door and turned to Sam. "Tell me what happened."

He told the truth. When he'd finished, she took his details and left the room without a word. She returned a few minutes later with a thick file in her hands. He read his name, stuck on the front. His criminal history. She slapped it down on the table and sighed. "Makes for some reading, that."

He eyed the folder. "Yeah?"

She crossed her arms and leant back in her chair. "So, what possessed you to come in today?"

"Don't know, thought it was the right thing to do. I told you the story. The whole truth."

"Got a bit of a history, haven't you, Sam?"

He stayed quiet. "Yeah, but I'm trying to do the right thing. I'm taking a plumbing course. Hopefully I'll be trained this time next year."

"And how've you been paying for that course?"

"You know, this and that."

"Stealing?"

"When I have to."

She shifted in her chair, tracing the rim of the table with her thumb.

His throat dried. "I swear I had nothing to do with that body. I just found it."

A glimmer sparked in the corner of her eye. She smiled. "Got a call from your block of flats. Britney Peterson. Name ring a bell?"

"Yeah, she's my neighbour."

"She saw you coming out of the building with the case in your hands. Blood dripping on the floor. There's a pair of officers looking the place over right now."

"I don't have nothing to hide."

She shrugged, rose from her chair and unlocked the door. "Maybe so, but we have to hold you."

"What?"

"You brought in a dismembered body. You're the prime suspect."

"I want to speak to Brian, my parole officer."

"On holiday."

"Officer Kite?"

She gritted her teeth. "Suspended."

3

A UNIFORMED OFFICER cuffed Sam, then led him along the corridor to the lockups. He shut him inside then left. The other cells were empty. A draught made him shiver. He pulled his knees to his chest and rocked back on the wooden bench. At some point, he stretched out and fell asleep, his teeth still chattering.

Heavy footsteps brought him round. He sat up straight and stretched. Since there were no windows, he had no idea what time it was. Detective Linton slunk into the lockup, then nodded for the uniformed officer to open the cell.

Sam blinked the sleep from his eyes. "What's going on?"

"We checked over the CCTV, and we have footage of you getting on the bus without the case, then off again, with it. At this time we're putting you on bail."

Sam stretched, then followed Linton back out through the police station. She walked with him to the steps outside, where it was dark.

"Don't go anywhere, okay?" she said. "If I get a whiff of you intimidating any witnesses or any reports of you stealing from innocent people, I'll drag you right back here."

"What about the killer?"

She sighed. "We don't know. Not yet."

4

S TANDING OUTSIDE the door of his flat, Sam fumbled his key, dropping it on the ground. It chimed against the hard surface, landing beside a dried patch of blood, from the suitcase. He would have to clean that later.

When he stepped into his flat, the smell of the dried vomit stung his nostrils. The puddle remained at the table. He breathed through his shirt. Aside from the vomit, something wasn't right about the flat.

A man stood in the corner, dressed in a suit.

Sam had presumed the detectives were finished. He just wanted to crawl into bed and forget he'd woken up this morning. "What do you want?"

"You stole my suitcase."

Then Sam recognised him. The businessman, from the bus. He stepped back, fumbling for the doorknob, but he slipped and fell, knocking his head against the wall.

The man approached, looming over him, cocking his head in the half-light. "You looked inside, didn't you?"

Sam nodded. "How did you find me?"

"Human bodies are heavy, aren't they? Difficult to run with them. I followed you home. You weren't very observant. Should take more care with your surroundings."

"I'm hardly a professional thief. I just need the money."

The man chuckled.

Sam scrabbled to his feet, but the man knocked him down. A sharp pain shot along his spine. He sucked air and grimaced.

The man pursed his lips. "Where is it?"

"Police have it."

The man's smile faded. He reached inside his coat and produced a knife. Its blade glinted. He edged closer.

"W—wait. I didn't tell them anything. They haven't a clue."

The man paused.

"Really," Sam said. "What could I tell them?"

The man grinned then stepped toward him. "It has nothing to do with getting caught. I wanted to take those remains somewhere special. Had a spot all picked out." He seized Sam's throat. "You'll just have to do instead."

Sam tried to scream, but his lungs emptied of air. He craned his neck downward. The knife stuck out just below his chest. His hands numbed, iced up. Warm blood gathered in a rivulet and ran into his belly button. He looked into the man's eyes and pleaded with silent words.

The man slipped his knife out of Sam, pulled back and jabbed again. He held his finger to his lips. "Shh, easy does it." He gestured behind him. "Check that out."

A set of tools: axes, saws, a hammer, and other items Sam couldn't name, rested on the table. At the table leg sat a brown suitcase, its upholstery peeling and a price tag still hanging off the handle.

The man drew back his arm and sliced Sam's throat.

Sam dropped to his hands and knees, feeling blood drain from him in crimson puddles. He coughed and spluttered, desperate to breathe.

A distant *thud*. Ringing. Then darkness.

COLD HEARTS

1

TERRY HILL FLIPPED his indicator and pulled off down into New Birchford. For the last fifty kilometres the green oil light had blinked at him through the gap in his steering wheel and he supposed he'd better get it checked out. It was his mother's car and this was the first time she had trusted him with it on such a long journey. If he messed up here she might not be so willing next time or, worse, ban him completely from using it.

Up ahead there was a blue and white police barrier in the road. He drove up to it, halted when he got in front of it and wrapped his fingers around the steering wheel, wondering what he should do. The stench of exhaust coiled up his nostrils. He was sure the car needed looking at. Aside from bringing it back in one piece he wasn't all that keen on it falling apart while he was doing a hundred kilometres an hour on the motorway.

He got out of the car, looked around the area, for some sign of a policeman, the source of this sign. Seeing none, he decided that it might just have been left there by accident. And this was a border-line emergency. If anyone asked him what he was doing, or questioned him about the sign, he would tell them about his car. They would agree he'd done the right thing. And, in any case, no one was around.

He slid the sign back from its place, its metal foundation grating the asphalt in something of an approximation of fingernails on a metal door. He crunched his teeth as he set it to one side, then got back in his car and drove on.

The high street rolled into view and Terry kept his eyes peeled for a garage. He leant over the wheel and stared out from beneath the windscreen. Nothing. He headed onward, glancing at the little oil light every few seconds, hoping that it might have disappeared and he could forget all about this, but whenever he looked back it was still there, glowing neon green.

He arrived in the centre of the town and parked the car up against the curb. He got out and peered around him. It appeared as if there were no one at all around. Only a couple of birds, flapping through the air, broke the image of stasis. He stretched his arms up over his head and then yanked out his mobile and dialled up Angela, his girlfriend.

Her voice sounded ragged and fatigued. "Terry? Are you okay?"

"Yeah, just stopped off to get the car looked over."

"What's the matter?"

"Light came on. Thought I'd better get it looked at, find a garage."

"Where are you?"

"New Birchford."

"Never heard of it."

"It's a small place."

She breathed gently. "Terry?"

"Yeah."

"I'm sorry about this weekend."

Terry screwed up his eyes and massaged his temples. "Nah, don't worry about it."

"I didn't want it to end up like it did."

Terry's mind tracked back over the dress up party. He had wanted to take Angela away somewhere, out into the countryside, together. But he had ended up getting stuck with her flatmates, another three girls. They'd dragged him along on a night out. He knew none of their names. There was a fat one, a loud, ugly one and a shy one. All of them just as boring as each other. He'd spent the whole evening thinking of constructive excuses to escape.

"No, no," he said. "It was all my fault. My responsibility. That was why I was calling. To apologise."

"Still, I feel bad about it."

"We had today together. That was enough, I guess."

"Kind of spoilt it being hung over, didn't it?"

"Nah," Terry said, shrugging. "It was fine."

Her calm breaths tickled his ear. "Terry?"

"Yeah."

"I love you."

Terry rolled his eyes and stared up at the flawless sky. Not a cloud. He scrunched up his expression and pressed his lips tightly together. "I love you too," he said.

Her voice brightened. "Call me when you get back home, okay?"

"Yeah," Terry said, and then ended the call.

He stuffed his mobile back in his pocket and absorbed his surroundings. Still no one in sight. Shops on the high street all shuttered up. Sure it was a Sunday, and this was a small town, but it seemed eerie that there were no inhabitants at all. Not even a dog walker, a jogger.

He checked over the street, looking for any sign of a pay machine, to buy a parking ticket. He picked it out, further up the road, and he saw that Sundays were exempt from charges. If the centre of town was like this every Sunday then he could see why.

Rolling his shoulders to loosen the tension in his neck, he marched on up the road, determined to find someone to help out with his car problem. He was sure that there must be a fair or something going on that day. There had to be a reason for no one being around.

After he had been walking for ten minutes, still without any sign of another person, he started to grow concerned. He couldn't remember the last time he had been in a public place so long without ever seeing anyone. It made him uneasy and he thought twice about having come here, having crossed over the police cordon. Perhaps it had been there for a very good reason.

A knot formed in his throat. Better to go back to the car. He backed up, headed back for his car, along the pavement. Soon he was running, fast. He bolted around the corner and the car appeared in his vision. And then, as he looked around once more, over the street, he caught sight of a person in a house, looking out through their front window, into the street. Right at him.

Terry hunched his shoulders and cast off his fears, laughing under his breath at how he'd acted like a kid, got scared and run off back toward the car. He approached the house, glanced at the person staring out, smiled at them, and then headed up to the door and rang the doorbell.

He waited at the door, listening for the footsteps. But they never came. He rang again, waited. Still nothing. He stepped back from the door. The person in the window remained there, staring out at him, or just beyond. He noticed they weren't making eye contact with him, keeping focussed on the middle distance, as if he weren't even there.

It wouldn't do to push himself onto this person, to get the police involved—if indeed there were any about—just because he wanted so desperately to speak to someone. So he slipped back and carried on down the street back to his car, deciding it better to leave the town and find a garage further along the route.

He got back into his car and fired up the ignition. He drove on through the high street slowly, not daring to gun the engine but also deeply afraid of the emptiness. When he drew level with the house where he had spotted the person and rang the doorbell, he noticed them still there, standing up and looking out, over the roof of his car. He gave a little sigh and then pressed the accelerator and bounded down the hill and away from the town.

No more than fifteen or twenty metres out of the town, the engine chucked and chortled. A thin plume of smoke weaved its way up from beneath the bonnet. Terry swore and then snapped off the ignition. He opened up and got out to inspect the damage.

He approached the bonnet, shovelled his fingers beneath it and lifted up. Smoke billowed out. Terry waved it away, clawing it out of his eyes and mouth. He stepped back and waited for it to clear. Although he knew absolutely nothing about cars he knew that the smoke wasn't a good thing.

The town bore down on Terry, up on its hill, the crooked buildings like jagged teeth in a rotten mouth. Did he really have any other option? He looked along the road that lead away from the town, in the direction he had been heading just now. There was nothing in sight.

Returning to the town carried certain benefits. For one he knew that there was at least one person there, he had seen them looking out through the window of their home. If he were to just keep on walking away he had no idea when he would come across another town. And so, turning his back on the smoking car, he headed back up the hill.

The town was just as it had been when he had left it a matter of minutes before. The streets were deserted and most of the shop windows were covered in metal gratings. Other theories leapt on him. An outbreak of infectious disease, a broken sewage pipe, a gas leak. All reasons that might see a town evacuated. But at least there was one person he could ask, get information on the situation.

He sidled along the street and arrived outside the house. He looked in through the window to see that now there was no one there.

A chill ran up his spine. He questioned his memory. He was certain that he had seen a person inside, looking out. He rubbed his eyes and looked again. No one was there. He tried the doorbell again but, as before, no one came to attend to him at the door. Reluctantly, he left the house behind and looked on through the town for some sign of human life.

Half an hour later the sun dipped behind the horizon, casting the whole town in shadow. He headed onward, trying desperately to find someone standing around but, as before, there was no one to find. When he reached the outer end of the town, from where he could make out the police barrier—still cast off to one side where he had left it—he turned around and doubled back, covering his same footsteps and ending up back in the town centre.

He picked out a wooden bench in the central square, underneath a war memorial, and he sat there, waiting for something to happen. He weighed his options. If he were to leave the town, head back down to his car, he would have to spend the night there. He didn't dare try to drive with it spitting smoke like that—he would be afraid that it might explode at any moment.

And then, across the square, he caught sight of someone. A brief flash of clothing and then they were gone.

The hairs on the back of Terry's neck prickled and he took off after the figure, calling out to them. He wound his way down narrow alleys, thinking to himself that he had caught sight of the person he was pursuing, only to realise that he had in fact seen no one and that he was running after thin air. Nevertheless, he beat onward until he wore himself out and had to stop to catch his breath.

"Are you lost?" someone said, behind him.

Terry wheeled around.

A short man stood there. He wore a long green anorak which brushed the tops of his shoes and a battered umbrella hat. Whiskers sprouted from his cheeks and his eyes were an icy blue. "Can I help you, stranger?"

Terry attempted to cast off his disbelief, to get his head around the fact that after all this time looking he had finally found a living, breathing human being. An oddly dressed human being, but a human being nonetheless. He attempted a smile but it came out more of a grimace. "Yeah, actually. It's my car. It's broken down. I could do with finding a garage."

"Ain't no garages round here."

"Oh?"

"Nope, afraid not."

Something about this man was unsettling, the way he kept up an unabating smile despite feeding Terry this news. Terry shrugged his shoulders and said, "Where is everyone?"

The man continued to stare.

Terry was on the cusp of asking the question again when the man suddenly lurched forward. Before he had time to react, he felt a sharp prick in his arm. He looked down at the site of the pain, seeing a needle slipping into his skin. His vision turned fuzzy and the world wobbled. Far away he felt his body drop away from his brain and collapse onto the cement.

2

TERRY'S BODY felt loose and inconsequential. His muscles felt warm and slippery, without power or coordination. He opened his eyes to see gloom pervading everything around him.

Somewhere in the distance water dripped out of a broken pipe, splashing on the ground and splattering into a puddle.

Terry tried to move his limbs and found them bound. He jerked from side to side, trying to get himself free but he had no give in the bindings. He called out into the darkness. His voice echoed back at him, bouncing off the walls and sending waves of nausea through his chest. His lungs prickled and he felt that he might pass out again at any moment.

Footsteps padded along the dank corridors, slapping and squelching.

Terry reeled his neck around, trying to catch sight of the figure approaching but his energy felt utterly sapped. He recalled the needle the man had stuck him with. It might have contained just about anything.

The man appeared close to Terry's side. He spoke in a whisper. His voice took on a hollowness that replaced the joviality from before. "Do you know where you are?"

Terry parted his lips to speak but the words dissolved on his tongue.

The man touched him on the arm. His fingers were rigid and leathery, like overcooked sausages. "You're underground, beneath the town."

Frantic, Terry tried to follow the man as he moved around him but he got disorientated and had to stop. His brain slopped against his skull and, almost of itself, his head nodded down onto his chest and he fainted once more.

3

A COLD DRAUGHT brought Terry round. He blinked away the sleepiness squatting on his consciousness and tried to get his thoughts straight, to stop them fizzing and bolting around from one end of his brain to the other. Now he was lying down. His back pressed up against a hard surface, stone. His muscles felt sore and cramped. He tried to move himself but the same sensation of stripped energy and physical ties around his arms and legs stopped him from doing so.

Tears dotted his eyes and scattered his senses. He felt so helpless and disorientated. None of the day had made any sense whatsoever. All he had wanted was to get the car fixed and be on his way. He wondered what time it must be right now, whether his parents would be worried that he hadn't yet arrived back home. That would surely save him from any harm. They would call the police, who would be able to identify his car using the security cameras on the motorway. They would find the car and this nutter would get into trouble. If they could find him.

As Terry's eyes got used to the darkness he started to be able to pick out basic forms. Some feeling returned to his neck muscles and he managed to get a look at the objects surrounding him. He made out another series of tables, just like the one on which he lay. On top of each were huddled forms. It took Terry another second to realise that they too, like him, were people, all brought down here.

He shifted his weight. "Hey? Can anyone hear me?"

No response.

The temperature in the room seemed to drop a couple of degrees. Terry shuddered. He wanted to bring his arms up to his chest, to cross them over his heart to keep himself warm. He spoke to the others once again, but received no reply.

Minutes passed. They might have been hours but he had no way of telling.

Slowly, Terry managed to get feeling back into his arms and legs. He could vaguely move them now. He had enough sensation in his arms to get hold of his binding, which turned out to be a thickly coiled rope, and managed to tug it free of his body. He listened for the dull *thud* as the rope snaked onto the ground, out of sight.

He wriggled his fingers and legs—they still felt unsteady, alien to the rest of his body, as if he had lost control of them. However, in the end, he worked up the courage to slide onto the edge of the stone table and set his feet on the ground.

He almost fell over as he stood up on his two legs. It reminded him of one of his cousins, a toddler, who would sway from side to side, looking certain to crumple into a heap but somehow, miraculously, always finding his balance right at the last moment.

He got over to one of the other tables and reached out to touch the person. Their skin was as cold as a midwinter frost and he jerked back his fingers. Another shudder passed through his body and he reflected that they must be in a freezer of some sort.

Last summer he had worked at a butcher's and they had had a storage room, out back of the shop. He recalled stepping out there to collect the cuts of meat and how the chill had burnt his skin and made his teeth chatter. Was that what they were now? Cuts of meat?

Not daring to touch the other person, he stalked his way around the room, finding his way around the wall to what appeared to be a doorknob. He clutched it in his fist and turned it, but it wouldn't budge.

From behind him he heard an elongated groan.

A tremor ran up his spine. He spun on his heel to look.

One of the bodies was moving around in the gloom.

Terry backed up from the door and headed over to the table, laying his hands on the cold stone and looking over the person, squirming about. "Hello? Can you hear me?"

The person murmured something which was impossible to discern.

"Sorry? What was that?"

Another moan, followed by a prolonged shaking of the ropes holding them down.

Hands trembling, Terry reached out and touched their skin. It sent a wave of cold through his nerves and he gasped. He snatched back his hand. As he stared longer and harder at the person he made out the white cloth covering their mouth. He tugged at the material, pulling it from the mouth and then dropped it on the floor.

The person wagged their head from side to side, coughed several times. The voice was female, young, maybe in her late teens or early twenties—the same age as Terry. "Here?" she said. "Is he here?"

"No," Terry said.

"Help me."

Terry stooped over the stone table and worked to free the ropes tying her down. When he got her free, he helped her off the table, onto her two feet.

She staggered around for a few moments before finding her balance again.

"Are you okay?" Terry said.

"I think so."

"What . . . what happened here?"

She gulped for air, reached out and steadied herself on the table. "Crazy. He's crazy."

"Who's crazy?"

"The artist."

"The artist?"

"He was given a commission for the town—to create a piece of art. But . . . but—"

The door squealed open and light flooded into the room.

Terry brought his arm up to shield his eyes from the brightness.

Above them a light bulb clicked on, adding to the light flooding in through from the corridor. The artist stepped into the room, only his silhouette visible. He halted, apparently staring at the two escapees.

"You!" Terry said.

The artist held an item in his arm, like a fire hose. The pipe snaked through his legs, back along behind him and back out into the corridor. Terry imagined that a smile must be spreading his lips. "You're awake," the artist said.

Not knowing how to respond, Terry stayed quiet. He felt the girl sidle up alongside him and touch him on the arm, duck behind him. She leant into his ear and whispered, "That . . . that thing. He's going to use it on us."

Terry ran his eyes over the fire hose once more, trying to establish exactly what it was for. He scanned the room again. The other people remained on their tables, lying still—sleeping on throughout this entire exchange. He would have to help them too, but first he had to help himself.

He slipped out from the girl's grasp and made for the artist, who raised the hose and pointed it in Terry's direction. He leapt through the air at the artist, his hands clawing at him and spittle bubbling in his throat.

The artist simply raised the hose pipe, aimed squarely at Terry and then released the valve.

Freezing mush pumped into Terry's face and soon covered his entire body. He felt his consciousness escaping him as he plummeted toward the floor. He opened his mouth to speak but he could produce no sound. As he lay on the ground, writhing in pain at the burning cold liquid, he caught sight of the artist's face as he loomed over him, a slight smile prying apart his lips.

4

WALTER FITSMAN had been commissioned for what was to be New Birchford's crowning glory. The piece of art which would define the town, give the whole place a centrepiece. He mumbled to himself as he put the final two figures into place, right beside the war memorial.

He positioned the man and woman in an embrace. Everything about the position of their bodies, how Walter had moulded them, worked well, showed them off as some kind of star-crossed lovers. He had got them into such a position so that they appeared as if they might not have seen one another for several weeks and this was their reunion. The only disappointment in this piece was the eyes. They were distant and cold, but there was nothing to do about it. You could only capture so much in art. There was a limit to what cold hearts could manage.

He stepped back from the figures, knowing that he had reached the end of his great artwork. Not only had he achieved what he had set out to do here—fulfilled his brief—he believed that this exhibition would be the defining work of his life.

He strolled his way up the street, heading up the hill so that he had a vista taking in the entire town. The town was scattered with figures, all around. People stood in the streets, as if they were conversing, while others sat on park benches or glanced out of their windows.

He let out a satisfied sigh. It had taken guile and no small amount of ether and formaldehyde, but he had got them all done. That boy, the one he had set in an embrace with the girl, had almost blown the whole work out of the water before he'd had a chance to finish.

Over the hills, in his ears, he could hear the lightness of sirens. He listened in on it and smiled to himself. He snatched up the hose pipe beside him, the tank still filled with liquid nitrogen and positioned it toward himself. They would remember him for this forever. He had put New Birchford on the map. He took in one final glance around at his greatest lifework and then kicked the tap and let it wash over him.

Author's Note

Thank you for taking the time to read one of my books. If you would like to hear about my latest releases you can sign up for my newsletter here: www.aviain.com

Thanks for reading!

AV Iain

Lost In The Dark
A Short Story Collection

Copyright © AV Iain, 2015.
Published by DIB Books
All rights reserved.

Cover design and layout copyright © DIB Books, 2015.
Cover art copyright © Bruce Rolff / Shutterstock, 2014.

This work is fictional. None of the characters or events depicted in this book are based on real life and any resemblance to real events or persons is purely coincidental. Neither this book, nor any part of it, may be reproduced without express permission from the publisher.

All rights reserved.

www.ingramcontent.com/pod-product-compliance
Lightning Source LLC
Chambersburg PA
CBHW031319280626
47169CB00019B/2142